PERIHELION

A Trilogy of Short Stories

Written by John Ballard Jr

Managing Editor Kristina Ballard
Editor Carla Matkin
With special help from Joshua Ballard

PERIHELION

First edition. July 12, 2023.

ISBN: 979-8223804925

Written by John Ballard.

Table of Contents

For more by the author, visit GroundedandSettled.net or scan the QR code below!

Also By the Author

Something to Brew On
Something Else to Brew On

Introduction

If you enjoy Christian science fiction, then I'm sure you'll enjoy this book. It spans across time and space in an adventure full of excitement, humor, romance and heartbreak. Come on the adventure that will keep you on your toes while in your seat reading it.

Part 1
Perihelion

Perihelion Chapter 1

"THE SUN IS DOING WHAT? GOING OUT! HOW DOES THE SUN GO OUT? DID SOMEBODY FORGET TO CHANGE THE BATTERIES?" exclaimed the General in disbelief.

"Well, that's not all....."

Let's not get too far ahead of ourselves. We need to go back a few days and catch you up.

It was a Thursday morning that started like any other morning on the shores of Galveston. Reggie was up early to get everything together and head off to work. Once he was ready, he enjoyed sitting on his balcony and feeling the wind coming off the Gulf while he sipped his coffee. He could sit there forever, eyes closed, smelling the fresh air as it kissed the face of the water and made its way to his balcony where it came to visit like an old friend. All the while the sounds of the waves' soothing serenade filled the atmosphere. It was by far the most relaxing part of his day. He'd then take a few moments to watch people starting their day jogging down the beach, or, like him, just sitting there and taking all of the natural beauty in. He loved watching people interact. Honestly, he just liked people. Living in a tourist town was great for him as it made it easy for him to meet all types of people.

Everything was wonderful, serene. The weather did seem a little off this morning, but Reggie really didn't think much about it.

Weather near the shore can seem a bit unpredictable at times. As he arrived at Zindwhich Industries, he had to pass all the usual security checkpoints to get in. "Hey Al, how's the misses?" he asked the security guard as he passed.

"Well, she is a little miserable carrying twins, but she is due any day now. It won't be long, now. Thanks for asking, Dr. Samuels," replied Al in a friendly and respectful voice.

"Absolutely, and Al, it's just Reggie." You see Dr Reginald Samuels is about the most down to earth scientist you'll ever meet. Not just any scientist, but a nuclear scientist. Which is why he worked at Zindwhich Industries in the first place.

As Reggie finally makes it to his office, he's greeted by the head maintenance man "Thorn." Now, his real name is Ray Hawthorn, but somewhere along the line he picked up the nickname Thorn. It has stuck ever since. "Hey, Doc, what's on the agenda today?"

"Hey, Thorn. Well, I gotta see what the General has up his sleeve. I'm sure it'll have something to do with Bigger Ivan," he chuckled.

To this Thorn responded, "You know he hates it when you call it that don't you?"

"Yes," said Reggie with a small laugh, "but that's what makes it so funny."

Bigger Ivan, as Reggie called it, was designed to be the biggest nuclear bomb ever created. Reggie was making reference to the Tsar Bomba or also called Big Ivan with his joke. This was the biggest nuclear weapon ever set off, which happened in the early sixties.

The nuclear bomb at Zindwhich Industries actually was called "The Game Changer" by most, though "BICTL238" was the technical name. It touted a 250-megaton capacity, along with a hydrogen bomb side, an atomic bomb side, and some new age technology that used different helium elements. This was the largest nuclear bomb ever made.

As Reggie started logging into everything, he pulled up the weather. This was a habit he had started before he even finished with school. "Well, folks, it looks like I got it wrong," said the weatherman on the TV mounted on the corner. "I know it's mid-June, but it looks like we're going to get a little cold snap." Now this began to pique Reggie's interest. This made no sense at all. He had been looking at the doppler radar himself, and nowhere had he seen anything that would suggest any upcoming cold weather. This was most peculiar indeed. The weather seemed to be changing into what could result in erratic changes down the road. They were small changes for now, but they didn't make sense. Not yet anyway.

"Dr. Samuels, report to Sector 6, Dr. Samuels, report to Sector 6," the intercom announced. "Now what?" exclaimed Reggie as he made his way to Sector 6, which is where The Game Changer was kept.

Upon arriving he was immediately met by the General. General Harwin Mather, to be more specific. He is a highly decorated retired 4 Star General. He stood about 5' 8" built out of pure strength and determination. He was a square jawed man with a squint-eyed stare that seemed to pierce straight into your soul.

"Dr. Samuels, what is the latest update on the project? I've got the heads of Zindwhich coming for a visit, and they would like to be brought up to speed."

"Good morning to you, too, General. Everything is on schedule. I've crunched all the numbers. Everything looks just right."

"Good then," says the General.

"I still have my concerns, General. I still don't understand why the company wants to make a bomb this size. I know they say that they have no intention of ever letting it be used in war, which is the only reason I signed up for this project in the first place. I just still don't understand why you would make something that you're going to pour this much money into if there is no profit, and they don't intend to use it."

"Dr. Samuels, you know why I was picked for this project? One is I take orders well and perform my job to the best of my ability. I am also good at keeping things moving in an orderly fashion. The other reason, and the most important, is that the owner of Zindwhich and I have been friends since elementary school. We trust each other completely. Trust, Dr. Samuels, that is the cornerstone of the friendship that Ethan and I share. If Ethan says he's not going to use it to harm people, then he's not."

"That's some friendship you have there, General. Not everyone is lucky enough to have not only found that type of friendship, but to have known each other that long is simply amazing. I just needed reassurance, and that's enough for me."

"Good then, I'll let them know everything is on schedule," said the General.

Ethan Conroy, the self-made multi-billionaire and philanthropist, was well known for his kind nature and humble character. He was born and raised in a small town in southern Mississippi. He grew up working hard and used that work ethic and his devotion to God to become what he is today.

Reggie returned to his lab to do some more investigation on this weather. Reggie was indeed a nuclear scientist, but he always enjoyed learning. This is why he was intrigued by the weather. He had been studying meteorology as of late. If there was something that he could study, he did.

Upon arriving back at his lab, he was met once again by Thorn.

Thorn: "Hey Doc. Man, I was on my online account and my followers are commenting about the weather being weird all over the world."

"Yes, Thorn, I've noticed it. I did not realize that it was that widespread, though. It may be nothing, but I do intend to look deeper into it. By the way, how many followers are you up to now?"

"Man, Doc, last I looked there were over 100,000."

"100,000!" Exclaimed Reggie. "That is very impressive."

"Well, Doc, you know I ain't really in it for the recognition. It's more about sharing Jesus. You can see Him in everyday life if you're just looking for Him. That's why I started the page in the first place. To encourage people to look for Him. To live by the premise 'what would Jesus do?' That's my goal. Not all of my followers are Christians, and there are many debates, but that's good."

"I do admire you, Thorn, and your dedication to God and spreading His love."

"Well thanks Doc. Anyhow, what about this weather?"

"Yes, let me investigate. If I figure anything out, I'll let you know."

As Reggie began to research, he did in fact verify that the weather was off throughout the world. It wasn't drastic, but it was indeed a weather phenomenon. For it to be so widespread, there had to be something that had changed. He began checking radars across the country. The news media was welcoming the cool snap. They kept saying it was a nice change from the heat wave that we'd been experiencing. Reggie on the other hand, wasn't sure what to make of it. He looked at the time and realized the visitors would be arriving soon. He would be expected to be there, so his research would have to wait.

As the executives began to arrive, the General was standing by to greet them. Suddenly, he hears an old, familiar voice.

"Hey there, Harwin. Been a bit hasn't it?" Mr. Conroy expressed.

"That it has, Ethan, that it has. How are the grand babies doing?"

"Doing well, how's Margaret? She just had a birthday, didn't she?"

"Yes, she did in March. Yours was the 4th of January if I remember correctly."

"That is correct," said Mr. Conroy as Reggie entered the conversation abruptly.

"That's around Perihelion Day!" Reggie says with a sense of pride for having known.

"Say what?" Pipes up the General.

"Perihelion Day -Mr. Conroy responds- it's the day that the earth is closest to the sun. It typically ranges from January 2nd to the 6th."

A look of surprise came over Reggie's face.

"You're not the only smart one around here. -says Mr. Conroy with a smile. - So, catch me up on the project."

The next few hours the team went over all the details of the status of the project. As the meeting concluded, all the executives loaded up and headed to the airport to go back to their respective homes and offices. Except for Mr. Conroy, he wanted to stick around a while and catch up with his old friend. Also, He wanted to be at the facility for a few days and watch how things were operating.

Thorn was just getting ready to test some new rocket boosters that were being considered for use on the project. Just as he was getting them into his shop, Mr. Conroy arrived.

"Hello, Thorn, good to see you again."

"Well, hello, Mr. Conroy, it is good to see you, too. I thought you were flying back with the rest of the bosses."

"Nah, I wanted to stick around for a few days. Would you like some help with these boosters? I still like to get my hands dirty."

"Sure."

As they worked on preparing the boosters for testing, they continued in conversation about anything that came to mind. Finally, the subject came up about Thorns mechanical arm and leg. He had lost his limbs when a young man who had been drinking, and driving ran him over while he was out jogging. This caused Thorn to lose his right arm and left leg. With advances in medical science and the technology at Zindwhich industries, which they kindly provided free of charge, a completely mechanical arm and leg were designed that replaced the lost limbs. Other than being able to see the metal of these limbs, one would never know that they were prosthetic.

"You know, Thorn, we have the capability to create a skin like material that we could put on the prosthetics that would make them look completely natural. Of course, for you, we'd do this for free."

"Thank you for the offer, Mr. Conroy, but I figure this is who I am. I figure if I spend my time trying to be something I'm not, then there's no time left to be me. Plus, seeing this is a reminder to me how God blessed me. I could have died; I may have not worked for such a generous company. Not only did y'all pay my medical bills, but you also provided these mechanical limbs for me. For that I am very grateful to God and to you."

"It was my absolute pleasure, Thorn. By the way, whatever happened to the young man that caused the accident?"

"Well funny you should ask that. You see that welder over in the other room?"

Looking through the tempered glass windows, Mr. Conroy saw the young welder that Thorn was talking about. "Yes, I do."

"Well," said Thorn, "that's him. I was able to get the court to drop all the charges, by getting him to work community service working with me at the homeless shelter. It also gave me the opportunity to minister to him and get his life turned around. He has become my assistant. He's now a certified welder and is one of my best employees."

"Thorn, that is amazing. I don't know many people that would have done that. That truly is a definition of mercy and grace. Mercy because you forgave him, but grace because you gave him what he didn't deserve."

"Well, sir, I can't just say What Would Jesus Do, I have to live it."

The two continued to talk as they finished up with the boosters. Once they were successfully tested, Mr. Conroy went back upstairs to make dinner plans with the General. As he arrived most people were wrapping up their day of work. Everyone, that is, but Reggie. He was still digging deeper into the weather phenomenon going on. He had just come down from the rooftop where there is a large telescope and communication equipment. Reggie was visibly shaken. He motioned for the General to come to his office. Mr. Conroy, observing this, joined them.

As they entered the room Reggie closed the door.

With a little shaking in his voice Reggie began to speak. "I do not know if you have noticed the weather being off, but it was bothering me, so I have been digging into it all day. What I have found is very disturbing. I know this is going to sound crazy, but you both know me well enough to know I've done the research. "

"Well spit it out man." Said the General.

"Well, um, the sun is going out. Like burning out."

"THE SUN IS DOING WHAT? GOING OUT? HOW DOES THE SUN GO OUT? DID SOMEBODY FORGET TO CHANGE THE BATTERIES?" exclaimed the General in disbelief.

"Well, that's not all. I was on the rooftop, in the observatory, to confirm my theory by using the telescope. When I heard radio chatter on the system that we have up there. I didn't really think anything of it at first but decided to respond to see who it was. Apparently, well apparently there is someone on the sun and they are reaching out for help. I know, I know it sounds crazy. So, I asked if they could give me some kind of proof that this was legit. They caused a series of solar flares seven in a row as proof."

Mr. Conroy with his eyes intently focused on Reggie says "So, you're telling us that not only is the sun going out, but that people live on the sun?"

Perihelion Chapter 2

First, let's get an understanding of the sun and its inhabitants. For the entire existence of the sun, the Zaya Race, which are the people of the sun, had kept everything working as designed. This was what they were instructed to do by the Creator in the beginning. The Zaya Race were not aware as a whole, but they had been facing the failure of the sun's functions for some time.

You see, the surface of the sun is more like an outer shell called "Exterius." The outer diameter of the sun is 864,000 miles. That is the part that is seen from earth. Inwardly, though, it is closer to 157,000 miles in diameter. This is still significantly larger than the earth at 7,917.5 miles.

The surface of what earth sees as the sun is actually the sky to the sun's inhabitants. Their sky from within though is a golden purple color. The vast majority of the heat of the surface always goes outward, thus it does not burn inwardly, burning up that which is within. There are giant cylinders called "The Columns" that reach from the center of the sun's core to the Exterius. These act as an insulated conduit of heat from the core to the Exterius. They are a two-part construction that work like a shell and tube heat exchanger. The heat feeds upward through the center or innermost part of the columns and unused heat travels back down through the outermost part of the columns. Because of this, the outermost part is the coolest part and regains some heat as it runs back down to the core. It also acts as an insulator so that the innermost part will maintain most of its heat, not being exposed to the cooler climate outside nor endanger the citizens around it.

The livable surface of the sun is called "Loca" and is watered from a dew that rises from underneath the ground. The loca is a very fertile ground that grows food well for the Zaya. There are no weeds or insects to compete with, so food is always in a plentiful supply. Though the food they grow is not just as earth's is. They have oceans, rivers, and many beautiful landscapes as well.

The Zaya had, since the dawn of time, faithfully taken care of their planet. They had advanced in technology in many ways beyond earth's technology in many but not all areas. They had long ago made flying vessels which are called "Volans," that had been made with the ability to fly through the Exterius. What this manifested to those of earth was a solar flare. The vessels were equipped with a cryogenic system that kept its occupants and cargo safe from the heat of the Exterius. The volans flew at extremely high speeds. This along with a map of wormholes is how they could move throughout the galaxy with ease. They also had a cloaking system that would prevent them from being detected by any type of tracking system that earth has. They came in a variety of sizes and capacities. The Zaya used these for exploring and studying Earth and its inhabitants. Through their studies, they had already learned every language on earth. It had been decided to not communicate with earth previously as the Zaya felt like Earth would see them as a threat, though they had come to earth over many years in disguise as part of their studies. They looked just like the people of earth, and their anatomy was the same. All they had to do was dress the part and try to blend in. The major difference between the Zaya and people of earth was that they lived much longer. Most lived to be around 400 to 500 years of age, though some lived longer. The oldest age that one had ever reached was 675. The oldest of Zaya were inducted into the "Counsel of Elders." Major decisions had to go through the Counsel before a final decision was made.

They had a thriving civilization with large cities and suburbs, just as earth. To power their technological advances including the volans they had placed large bands around the columns. The bands absorbed heat from the columns and generated it into energy. Unfortunately, though, this began slowly to reduce the outermost heat that was returning to the core. With that it also affected the innermost heat as well. It was an extremely slow downward spiral that didn't really get noticed until it was too late, by most.

The Zaya were a peaceful people for the most part. That is, they were not aggressors, but they were very untrusting. This had made them refocus from what they were supposed to be doing. Instead of maintaining their planet, they had begun to focus on making sure they were prepared in case of attack. They did not take into account that the Exterius was actually their best defense if maintained properly. They had the only technology that could go through its heat.

There was a brilliant young scientist whose name was Arliaya. Her intelligence and tenacity were matched only by her beauty. She had already noticed the irreversible damage that was being made by the actions that they were taking. She had many times approached the Counsel about the effects that had been taking place. Unfortunately, the Counsel had not heeded her warnings. The changes were so minute that they did not see the harm.

It also didn't help that Fortius, who was a strong and courageous leader with a 6' 5" frame and a physique that looked as if it had been chiseled out of stone, passionately opposed her every attempt. He always had the Zaya and their best interest in heart but was blind to the damage that was happening. He was very zealous in bettering their civilization. It was he more than any other that wanted to make sure that they were protected. For he had no trust at all for the people of Earth and thought, given the chance, Earth would go to war. This is because he himself had done much research on earth and its inhabitants. He saw how often they were at war amongst themselves. He wondered if they were this way among their own kind, how much more with those from another planet?

After one such occasion they met in the counsel halls afterwards.

"Arliaya, Arliaya!" Fortius called out. "Arliaya wait! I wanted to talk to you."

"Well, you're good at that aren't you Fortius. It's listening that isn't your strong suit." Quipped Arliaya.

"Arliaya, I want you to know that I am not trying to discredit you. I just honestly don't think that your concerns are that serious. I think maybe you should take another look at your data. Maybe you have made a minor mistake that you've overlooked."

"Fortius, don't you think I've gone over the data multiple times before I brought it to the Counsel. I wouldn't bother them with this if I wasn't absolutely sure. I am just trying to protect everyone."

"That's what I'm trying to do, too, Arliaya. Can't you see that?"

"Fortius, I see that you care for our people and our well-being. I think though you're so focused on what you think is the right way, that you're blinded to anything other than that. Why not come to my lab, I'll show you the results. If you went to the Counsel with me, they would believe me."

"I'm sorry Arliaya, I don't think..."

"Exactly, you don't think. You act. Eventually your actions may cost us everything. Then what, Fortius?"

At this Arliaya stormed off. She was furious because she too loved her people and wanted the best. She just couldn't get through to them. If she didn't change their minds soon, it may very well be too late.

Fortius walked away. He didn't believe that Arliaya was right, but what she said struck a chord with him. What if he was wrong and could have done something? He could possibly be responsible for the destruction of his own people. He decided to visit the columns and do a little research of his own.

Back in her lab Arliaya was busy trying to piece together a timeline of how rapidly the cooling process was taking place. She thought, she hoped, maybe she could come up with a way to stop it or at least slow it down. She was at the point of grasping for straws. Tears began to well up in her eyes and run down her cheeks. She so desperately wanted to help her people but didn't know how.

"Daughter, what is bothering you that has brought you to tears?" Asked her father Milo as he entered the room.

"Father, I just don't know what to do. I'm afraid our planet is in grave danger. I've tried to convince the Counsel but to no avail." She said through her tears.

"Hmm" pondered Milo. "Have you talked to the Creator about this?"

"No, I have not, father."

"If there is something that you cannot change, then you should talk to the Creator. He can give you direction on how to approach it, or He will change it Himself."

"Yes, father, I just got so busy and tied up trying to fix this, that I guess I forgot."

"That is where most of our problems come from, forgetting the Creator and ultimately our purpose."

"You are absolutely right, father. Thank you for that."

"It's my pleasure. By the way, here's your lunch. You forgot that too." Milo said with a chuckle.

"Thank you again. I love you!"

"I love you too, daughter."

As Milo left, Arliaya knelt to pray and ask the Creator for help.

Meanwhile Fortius was investigating for himself. Knowing full well his way around the Columns, he began to take temperatures and flow readings. Much to his surprise the temperature was much lower than it should have been. Plus, the flow was decreasing. He knew if it was this way here, it would be much worse at the Exterius. A panic set in as he realized that Arliaya was right. He may have doomed his people and planet for being so bull headed. He leaped onto his transport vehicle that he had ridden out to the site and raced to see Arliaya.

As Arliaya was just rising from prayer Fortius burst in the door.

"Arliaya, Arliaya you were right. Oh, what have I done? We have to do something. Please, what can we do?"

"Fortius, what happened? Why this sudden change of heart?"

"I thought about what you said. I thought what if I was wrong, and I was. I took readings. I even ran them past a friend of mine. It's not good. I don't know what to do."

"Calm down Fortius. First stop and breath. We need to remember our Creator and ask for His help." They took a moment to pray as Arliaya led. "Oh, wise Creator of all things, we ask that you give us guidance and help. Let your face shine upon us. Amen."

"Amen."

"Okay, let's go."

Away they went as fast as they could. Upon arrival they begged to see the Counsel immediately. Once in front of the Counsel they explained thoroughly what was happening. They expressed the urgency of immediate action.

The Counsel was first taken back by the two but having them both agree and explain everything to them made them realize that things really were dire. As they finished up, the Counsel responded.

"Ultimately, what has gone wrong is we have forgotten our purpose. The Creator put this planet in our care. We have been more focused on our comfort and safety than our purpose. We must amend this error. Now, do you know how to fix the damage done?"

"I'm afraid this is where it gets a little more complicated." Said Arliaya. "We have made great advances in technology, but I do not know that we have the technology or resources here to fix this."

"What are you suggesting Arliaya?" Asked the Counsel.

"We are going to have to reach out to Earth for help."

"THE EARTH?"

"Yes, though unorthodox and highly irregular..." Arliaya started to say but was cut off by the Counsel.

"Highly irregular? We've never reached out to the earth."

"I know," stated Arliaya, "but I don't think we have any other choice."

The Counsel began to murmur amongst themselves.

Then Fortius spoke up. "Excuse me, I would like to speak. Everyone knows how I feel about the Earth, and how I do not trust its inhabitants. You all know the great strides I have implemented to make sure we were protected from them. I wanted to protect our people and our planet from what I saw as a threat. Yet, what I didn't realize is that our greatest threat was from within. We have successfully doomed ourselves and in doing so we have doomed Earth as well. We were the threat. Without any advances against us, we have placed a death sentence on the people of Earth. We failed to realize that our Creator is theirs as well. That makes us a type of kindred. So, we can now sit and do nothing and watch two worlds die, or we can listen to Arliaya, which we should have done a long time ago. I say we reach out. At this point, what is the worst that could happen?"

With this said it was unanimously agreed to contact earth.

Perihelion Chapter 3

Back in the observatory, Reggie was keying up the communication system to try and reconnect with the sun. The General, Mr. Conroy, and Thorn stood by intently watching and listening.

"Hello, hello?" Reggie spoke into the microphone. "Hello, is there anybody there?"

A voice came from the other end. "Yes, we are here." Arliaya replied.

The others in the room's eyes grew wide in disbelief.

With a slight shake in his voice Reggie began. "My name is Dr. Reginald Samuels. I am here with some colleagues. We are pleased to speak with you."

Arliaya replied "I am Arliaya, I am a scientist here on what your people call the sun. I am accompanied by Fortius, a leader of our people, the Zaya. We thank you for responding to our message."

"Yes, yes, indeed. It is our pleasure." Reggie answered. "I do have to say that we are honestly very surprised. We did not know that there were people on the sun. We didn't even think that could be possible with all of the heat."

"Well, on the sun may not be exactly right. It's more like in the sun." Arliaya took some time to explain the Exterius and the Loca of the sun. She explained how the heat did not affect those living within. This idea greatly intrigued Reggie.

"How very interesting. Can you explain how this is? I cannot quite wrap my head around this." Reggie asked.

The next few hours were spent with Arliaya explaining the situation on the sun in full detail. Answering all the questions that Reggie asked. The two scientists from different worlds communicated everything they could so a solution could be reached. Arliaya explained thoroughly how their planet worked to Reggie, as well as why they were in the situation they were in now. As the conversation crept into the morning hours, Thorn made sure the coffee stayed brewing.

At one point Reggie expressed, "I just really wish I could actually come there and run tests with my equipment. That way I could better understand what to do. Not that your tests are inadequate, but we use different technology and testing methods making my ability to interpret them less adequate. The problem is getting there."

Fortius spoke up, "That's not a problem. I can come get you and your equipment."

This stunned everyone sitting in the office. "Really? That's possible?"

"Absolutely, no problem." Fortius as if this was a trivial issue, which to them it was. He explained how the volans worked in detail reassuring Reggie that it was safe.

Thorn also volunteered to go with Reggie as he, being a mechanic, could also be of assistance. Finally, they signed off and agreed to reconvene at a set time the next day. This would give Reggie time to gather the equipment he needed. As they signed off, there was a sense of uneasiness in the air, for all involved.

Arliaya and Fortius reported everything to the Counsel in full. Then, once everything was cleared and set, Fortius began to prepare a Volan for travel. For the first time in a long time, Arliaya felt hopeful. She thought maybe, just maybe, they might be able to pull this off and save everyone.

Back on earth, Reggie spins his chair around facing everyone for the first time in hours. He lets out a deep sigh, leans back in the chair as he runs both hands through his hair, gripping the strands as if to take a grasp on his brain and let it settle for a second.

Mr. Conroy breaks the silence. "Reggie, are you alright?"

Reggie slowly sits forward and runs his hands down his face taking a slow breath in and exhaling even slower. Finally, after truly assessing himself, he says: "I think so, I don't know, I, it's just, it's just so much to take in."

"Breath Reggie, it's a lot, but you're not alone. We've got a good team. Plus, I have contacts all over the world. So, if we need more help, I'll get it."

"Thank you for that. We've got a lot to do. I'm going to gather everything I think I may need, though what that maybe I'm not really sure. Thorn, I suggest you do the same."

Thorn replied, "I was just fixing to suggest the same thing."

The two hurried off to gather everything they thought they might need. They weren't even sure what to bring to the sun. This was completely uncharted territory, and they didn't have the time to sit and deliberate over what all could happen and how to prepare.

The General and Mr. Conroy were left there alone. They looked at each other intently. The General started, "So, life on the sun, huh?"

Mr. Conroy responded "Yeah, really didn't think that was a conversation we would ever have. Long way from two boys growing up in Mississippi."

"That it is, that it is."

"Well, I guess I need to make some phone calls. I probably should call the President first, then we'll contact the rest of the world's leaders. These will be some interesting conversations to say the least."

"I'll call my contacts at the Pentagon."

With that they parted ways.

Reggie frantically gathered everything he could think of to take with him. He ran from his lab to his office and back again. He finally reached the point that he thought he had everything. He hurried home to grab extra clothes and essentials. At one point, he sat down just to breathe. Because he had been rushing around so much, he had been awake for over 24 hours. He was just making a list in his head of everything when he dozed off. He was startled awake thirty minutes later by a severe weather warning going off. The weather changing temperatures back and forth so quickly was causing storms worldwide. He thought to himself, "We've got to hurry." He grabbed his bag and headed out.

Back at the lab everyone was bustling around trying to get everything in order. Thorns assistant was helping him put together the last of his things.

"Are you really going to the sun," Thorn's assistant asked. "Isn't it dangerous?" With all Thorn had done for him, his assistant really looked up to and cared for him. He did not want to see any harm come to him.

"Yes, we are going to the sun. Whether it's dangerous or not, I don't know. Honestly, it doesn't matter if it is. If we do nothing, the sun might go out, and if that happens, we all die. So, even though I don't know if it's dangerous to go, it's more dangerous if we don't."

Reggie had arrived back to the lab, and it was now time to get back in touch with Arliaya. They all gathered in the observatory, equally nervous and fascinated. They started up the communications system and Arliaya and Fortius were standing by. Reggie informed them that they were ready to go whenever they were.

Fortius told them that he could be there in less than 12 hours. This amazed everyone in the observatory. With all they had learned and encountered in the last twenty-four hours, however, they didn't even question it. They had some more conversation and gave Fortius their exact coordinates. They signed off again and began to talk it over.

The General said, "So, now we wait."

Mr. Conroy suggested everyone try to get some sleep as this was going to be a long process. They also had an online summit with the world leaders in just 5 hours, so they needed to be rested. Everyone went to their offices to try and rest. It was hard to settle, but soon the lack of sleep set in on them all causing them to crash hard. Rest didn't last long, though. Just a few short hours later they were all up getting ready for the online summit.

There was a frenzy of excitement, fear, and apprehension in the air as the world leaders were just now finding out all of this new information. Zindwhich industries had set up the online summit to update the world leaders. Zindwhich had first contact, not to mention some of the best technology to communicate with the Zaya, so it only made sense to let them take the lead on this.

As all the leaders came up on video the room filled with a chaotic flow of questions and confusion as everyone overlapped each other as they tried to speak all at once.

"Are they the enemy?"

"What do they want?"

"Why are they contacting us now?"

"The sun is going out?"

"Is this a joke?"

It was quickly becoming more like a volcanic eruption than a meeting. The communication team members that were running everything were visibly shaken. Seeing the way everything was going, Mr. Conroy simply reached over and muted everyone but himself. There were definite benefits to virtual meetings

"Good evening, distinguished guests and leaders. I thank you for all tuning in to this summit. I know there are many questions. We plan on addressing them, but we must do it orderly. To prevent confusion, you will see a message board across the bottom of your screen. This is where you can type in and submit your questions to be reviewed by our team. I hope that most of your questions are answered by our presentation. Let us remember these are trying times. We must all pull together as one to get what needs to be done, accomplished. Not just for ourselves, but for our children and their children. We must, I repeat, must work together to save the sun and our world. With that being said, I would like to present to you the man that made this discovery. Dr. Reginald Samuels."

As Reggie starts to step up in front of the camera to speak, his nervousness is nearly tangible.

The General leans over and whispers. "Reggie, you've got this. You are the most brilliant man I know. Do not let a bunch of politicians on computer screens intimidate you. Get out there and show them what you're made of."

This gave Reggie the boost of confidence that he needed. He spent the next few hours explaining what he and his team knew at the time. He explained that the sun was definitely going to go out if something wasn't done. From his observations, it appeared now that it may take weeks or possibly months before it went completely out. If, or rather when, the sun did go out, it would be a very short time before the earth froze, and that was if the worsening storms didn't destroy everything first. He informed everyone that a transportation ship was on its way to get them. Once they had gone to the sun and gathered more data, they would hopefully find a solution.

Mr. Conroy stepped in at this point. "Dr. Samuels, on behalf of everyone, I'd like to thank you for your presentation and efforts in this. We do not want to keep you any longer. We know you have more important things to do than go on about this all day."

From this point Mr. Conroy addressed the leaders. "I do want to assure you all that we have all the best minds in this. We will reach out for any help we need. I suggest that you communicate with the public as to what is going on but try to not bring the world into hysterics. I am positive that between our team here and the team on Zaya, we will come to a solution to save both of our peoples. We will be using Mr. Hawthorn's online account to help keep everyone informed as it already has a large following. As a symbol of transparency, we have equipped Mr. Hawthorn with a couple of very high-tech cameras that he has linked to his online account. He will be providing a live video feed of everything going on. You and the world can go to his account and stay updated, the address should be on your screen now. If you are a praying person, now would be the time to pray. If you are not, now would be a good time to start. With that, I thank you for joining us."

Reggie looks at Thorn and says, "You're fixing to get a lot more followers."

Thorn just smiles and says, "It looks like it."

With this, the summit concluded, and the rest awaited the arrival of Fortius.

Fortius began to approach earth. He radioed ahead to let them know he was getting close. He then slowed his ship down so they could see him on radar and follow his arrival. He did this to gain their trust and also so they could help guide him if he got off course. It wasn't long until a crowd had formed outside the facility to catch a glimpse of the visitor from the sun. The whole world had their eyes to the skies.

Fortius soon arrived at the facility. As he landed, there was an anticipation in the air that you could almost breathe in. Mr. Conroy had limited the first meeting to a handful of people so as to not intimidate Fortius. Just as Fortius was trying to gain Earth's trust, Mr. Conroy was trying to gain his. As Fortius exited his ship everyone gazed with a slight tremble inside. Some of excitement, some of fear, and some for just an overflow of emotions. Fortius walked straight up to the crowd and stretched out his hand as a friendly gesture. Shaking hands was a common greeting on the sun, as well, and a trait he learned Earth appreciates from previous studies of the planet.

Mr. Conroy was the first to greet him. "Hello, my name is Ethan Conroy. It is my absolute pleasure to make your acquaintance. I would like to formally welcome you to Earth. Anything that you need, we will do our very best to tend to."

Fortius responded with "Thank you, it's my pleasure. It is my hope that we can help each other."

"Agreed." replied Mr. Conroy.

Soon everyone was shaking hands and greeting Fortius. Once he greeted most of the others, he met Reggie. Reggie was so excited to meet him he almost spoke in fast forward.

"Hello, I'm Reggie, um Dr. Samuels, but everybody calls me Reggie. I'm so very glad to meet you! Thank you for coming and thank you for reaching out. Did I mention I'm really excited to meet you?" Reggie sounded as excited as if he had just met his all-time favorite celebrity. To be fair, though, this experience was a much less likely occurrence.

With this Thorn placed his hand on Reggie's shoulder and reached to shake Fortius's hand. "Calm down, Doc, you're going to scare the man off. I'm Thorn, pleased to meet you myself. That's a nice ship you got there."

Fortius responded "I am very glad to meet you all. I would love to stay and chat, but we have more pressing matters to attend to. We must get loaded and head back immediately."

The statement brought forward the situation once again. Almost in unison everyone said "Yes, yes."

So, everything was loaded up. They said their goodbyes quickly and headed off to the sun.

Perihelion Chapter 4

Reggie and Thorn looked on as they traveled towards the sun like two little children. They were amazed at how fast they were going, not to mention the fact that they were going in and out of the wormholes. It was all such an experience they could barely contain themselves. The cameras were capturing what they could of this, but everything was moving so fast. The cameras were installed on devices that acted like drones that continuously hovered near Reggie and Thorn. The two men were wearing trackers on their wrists that were synced to the cameras, so they always stayed near them.

Eventually, Thorn and Fortius began conversing over the Volan and how it worked. They spent some time talking over its details. As a mechanic this was of great interest to Thorn. The trip went quickly, mostly because of all the excitement and wonder. Before they knew it, they were approaching the sun. As they got near, it was like a snap of the finger, and they were through the Exterius.

What they beheld next made everything they had seen before seem less significant. The beauty that was before them as they scanned over the planet and all its components was breathtaking. The Columns protruded up and looked like the reddest part of a fire with just small hints of gold. The loca and its plants and landscaping were a sight to behold. It was like you'd taken the most beautiful colors and painted the ground in an intricate and delicate pattern. As they approached their landing, they finally looked up and saw the sky. It was a brilliant dark purple with a golden backdrop. It was as if one had taken liquid gold poured in purple paint, then sat it on fire. They were just taken back by everything.

Once they landed, they began to exit the ship. Fortius had already let them know that the atmosphere was like that of earth and was breathable to them. The Counsel were the first to meet Reggie and Thorn. They were very pleased that they had agreed to help. Not only that, but they were willing to come to the Zaya's planet to do so.

Just as they were finishing up, Arliaya approached. Reggie was immediately mesmerized by her beauty. In his eyes, she was more beautiful than anything he had encountered already, it all simply paled in comparison. As he stared Thorn leaned over and said, "Blink Doc and pick your chin up off the floor."

"Oh sorry, thanks," replied Reggie. He then regained his composure and greeted Arliaya. "You must be Arliaya, it is very nice to meet you in person."

Arliaya replied, "Yes, I am. It is very nice to meet you as well. Thank you for making the trip to help. I hate to rush into work, but we must be hasty."

"Absolutely. Where do we start?"

Arliaya and Fortius brought them to one of the Columns. Here Reggie began to analyze the Column and the soil around it. As he was doing this, he shared an observation.

"I don't mean to overstep any, but if you don't mind, I have a couple suggestions."

Arliaya replied "by all means, share."

"Well, I've noticed these blankets or bands I think you called them. As you've noticed, they are taking away power from the columns, lessening the effectiveness of the system in place producing your Exterious. You know, there is a way to utilize the power coming from the columns without drawing any away. At Zindwhich, we have a new type of solar panel that absorbs light and radiant heat. You could place them far enough away that there would be no negative impact on the Columns. That is if we can fix the problem at hand."

"That is a wonderful idea! So, we could get the same results without harm. That would be so great!"

"Yes, I have also been working on pressure pads that can be placed in high traffic areas, be they foot or vehicle traffic. They convert the pressure applied to electricity. These two sources of power should more than make up for what the bands produce."

"Would it be possible to put the pads on the bottom of shoes or transportation vehicles to maximize use?" Arliaya asked.

"That is an amazing idea, truly. I'm sure it could work. We will have to look into these after we fix this."

Arliaya agreed. They tirelessly worked looking at every detail they could. Somehow, they needed to kind of jump start and re-energize the core. Too much heat had been taken and merely shutting down everything that was pulling from it, would not stop it. The core needed its heat replenished. But how? They weren't sure yet, but they knew this was a must. They thought about trying to reheat the Columns with hopes that the heat would transfer. Unfortunately, though, all of them would have to be reheated at once, and it would take entirely too long for the effect to take place. Regardless, they weren't capable of producing enough heat to actually make that work even if they had all of the time in the world.

What they needed was the ability to directly access the core somehow. They could not go through the Columns. They were nearly impenetrable. Even if they did happen by some miracle to penetrate one, it would rupture, and the flame would blow out of the hole. They couldn't go through the top because the intense heat would be constant. Not even a Volan could make it from top to bottom before it was destroyed. So, they concluded that they would have to go through the ground. That had its own challenges. How could they get through the ground fast enough to make a difference?

After some time deliberating their options. Thorn suddenly spoke up. "I've got an idea. We have a tunnel boring machine back at Zindwhich that we were working on. We call it the Ditch Digger. It is drivable, and as it bores through the ground it fills the hole in behind it. Or at least that's what it's supposed to do. We've actually never tried it. The only problem is that it is a slow-moving machine. It would take a long time to get to the core."

"Maybe we could somehow combine it with a Volan or at least the technology and get to the core quicker?" Said Fortius.

Thorn was excited about the idea. "That's right up my alley! I can help with that."

Reggie thought about this and said, "Yes, Thorn, that may work. We still have to figure out how to reheat it though. We will need to contact Mr. Conroy and the team to see what options we may have. Fortius, do y'all have a Volan big enough to transport the Ditch Digger back here?"

Fortius replied "I'm sure we do. Just need the dimensions. We have larger transport Volans that can easily transport larger objects."

"Great," replied Reggie.

They decided to head back to the city. On the way, Arliaya and Reggie struck up a conversation.

"Reggie, I have studied Earth for many years. I would love to talk to you about it. Maybe I could learn more from you? I love to learn, and Earth has become an interest of mine."

"It would be my pleasure to help you with that. I too love to learn so I'd like to learn more about your planet as well," Reggie answered excitedly

"That's a deal." The pair smiled at each other, satisfied with the deal they struck.

As they returned, a feast had been prepared to share the gratitude of the Zaya for the help they were receiving. Alexander, the eldest of the Counsel, addressed everyone.

"We, the Zaya, would like to show some token of thanks for the help of Dr. Samuels and Mr. Hawthorn. They have traveled far, voluntarily we might add, to help a people that they do not know."

Thorn couldn't pass the opportunity up. Quietly, so he didn't interrupt the Counsel, he turned to the camera and said, "That's what Jesus would do."

The elder continued, "We commend your bravery and give you thanks for your assistance. May the Creator shine upon us all and bless this endeavor to be a success. We also thank you, oh great Creator, for this food before us. For it is through your blessings that we have received it. May you always be exalted." With this Alexander nodded his head and gave a slight wave of his hand to give permission for the feast to begin.

Thorn piped up, "Man this looks delicious. Good food, good meat, Good Lord, let's eat."

Arliaya wasn't pleased with stopping work, but knew that they needed to eat, lest they become too weary. Also, she knew if the Creator was helping, then a pause to eat would not hurt.

Thorn, Fortius, Reggie and Arliaya were all seated together. They spoke of many things. Fortius and Thorn were going over how to combine their machinery.

Meanwhile, Arliaya and Reggie were gleaning information off of each other. It was really the first time that Arliaya had stopped to really enjoy a conversation in a long time. She had a glisten in her eye and a smile on her face. As she and Reggie talked, she could feel something welling up in her that she had never felt before. She had never enjoyed talking to someone else so much.

The feast went on for some time. Fortius and Thorn had already left to take measurements of a Volan and draw out how to make these two machines one.

Reggie and Arliaya were lost in conversation. The impending problem had slightly faded from their minds. They were getting lost in learning from each other and learning about each other. They both spoke of the beautiful sights of each world. Reggie tried to explain watching the sun rise over the gulf.

"Close your eyes. Imagine you're sitting in darkness. You can feel the wind blowing off of the water. It smells fresh and crisp as it gently blows all around you. You hear the birds as they seemingly call for the rising of the sun. Then you see it. It's the most beautiful sphere of fire peeks over the edge of the water. Like a child peeking around the corner to see if you're there. Then within minutes, the sun is up. You can see clearly, and a new day has started. That's how I see ideas. Like the sun rising over the gulf. You first catch a glimpse of an idea. Then if you just focus on it, before long, you can see clearly."

Arliaya had never heard anything like this. Not only did she love Reggie's vivid description, she was quickly falling in love with him. She kept trying to shake it, but it had a grip on her that she couldn't resist.

Reggie was feeling the same way, though. He had never felt like talking to someone else had been so easy and yet so difficult at the same time. They began to walk to her lab as they talked along the way. Once they made it to the lab. They tried to think of how to generate enough heat to re-energize the core.

Thorn and Fortius arrived about that time. They decided to contact Zindwhich and see if they could all come up with something together. As the call went through the General was there waiting.

"Hello," said the General. "Is all well?"

Reggie responded "Yes and no. We've looked at the data, and we have to somehow get to the core of the sun. We are hoping to use the Ditch Digger there at Zindwhich. We will have to transport it here, then combine it with a Volan to give it the speed needed. Once we reach the core, we'll have to generate enough heat to re-energize the core. We're still working on that though."

Mr. Conroy, who had just entered the room, spoke up. "Reggie how much sleep have you gotten in the last couple of days?"

Reggie replied back, "Not much Mr. Conroy. I've just honestly been so busy, and so much has happened that there just wasn't enough time to sleep."

"I do understand that. Do you know that a lack of sleep can affect your cognitive performance? Even with someone as smart as you. God designed us that way."

"Yes, sir, I am aware. I've just been so busy."

"Again, I understand, you've got a lot going on. I'm going somewhere with this though. You're so tired and focused on the problem that you can't see the solution. You're too zoned into it. The good thing is you're not alone and have plenty of help. Remember you're not the only smart one around here." Mr. Conroy said with a chuckle.

"Yes, sir, I just..."

Mr. Conroy cut Reggie off. "Son, what you need here is a game changer."

Reggie's eyes came wide open, and his face brightened. As all of a sudden, he realized what Mr. Conway was trying to get through to him.

"YES! YES! That will work! Why didn't I think of that sooner? Oh, man, that's, that's perfect. That, I mean, that. Mr. Conroy, thank you! Yes, we will send transports that way as soon as they can leave. Why didn't I think of that? Man, my brain must be fried. Yes.."

The General stepped in, "Reggie, calm down, and let's get this show on the road. We'll be preparing everything here that y'all need."

"Yes, sir, General. Thank you, thank you again Mr. Conroy." With that he signed off.

He turned to look at the others. While Arliaya and Fortius stood there looking confused, Thorn just had a huge smile on his face and said, "So we're going to put a nuclear bomb into the sun."

Perihelion Chapter 5

Reggie explained everything to Arliaya and Fortius about the Game Changer and how a nuclear bomb worked. Meanwhile, everyone was rushing around trying to get everything ready on both planets.

On the sun, Volans were being prepared for transport.

On earth, the Ditch Digger was being serviced to make sure everything was in working condition. Once a thorough inspection of the vehicle was completed, it was stationed in position to be loaded. The Game Changer was being carefully and meticulously packaged so it could safely be transported.

The General and Mr. Conroy began to talk everything over.

"So, Ethan, you think this will all work?" The General asked.

With confidence, Mr. Conroy answered, "Yes Harwin, I know it will."

"I appreciate the confidence there, but let's not count our chickens."

Mr. Conroy sighed at his friend's lack of faith. "It's not about counting chickens Harwin, it's about trusting God. You've never really asked me why I decided to build this bomb."

"No, I trust you. You told me that you weren't going to use it on people, so I trusted that. Don't tell me you knew that you were going to put it in the sun."

"No, I didn't, but God did tell me to build it. I kinda felt like Noah building the Ark. It didn't make sense to anyone around me. Thankfully, though, everyone I needed to complete this project just fell in place. I guess that's how the animals came to the Ark. They just showed up and fell in place. Interesting now that I think about it."

"So, you're telling me that this whole time you had no idea what this thing was going to be used for? You just built it because God told you to?" The slight incredulity in the General's voice was barely masked by the awe he had for his friend. It took a lot of faith to embark on something like this without having an inkling of what it was going to be used for.

"Yep."

"Ethan, that's a little crazy. I mean, I'm glad you did because it obviously worked out."

"Well, Harwin, faith can be a little crazy at times."

Reggie and those with him were just as busy on the sun. There were countless helpers working to get everything in place.

Reggie was going through a list of things that he wanted Thorn to tell Mr. Conroy and the General once he got back to pick up the equipment they needed..

Thorn stopped him, "I don't mind telling them, but why don't you tell them when we get there?"

"I'm not going with you, Thorn. I think I can be a better help here getting things prepared for you when you return."

"Okay then, I guess that does make sense. So, what did you want me to tell them? You know what, why don't you write it down." Thorn knew Reggie well enough to know the list was likely going to be longer than his memory would allot for.

"That's a good idea," Reggie responded with a nod, thinking the same thing.

Fortius was directing his crew of mechanics on what they were going to need from the Volan that was going to be combined with the Ditch Digger. This way, they could have everything in place for when it arrived. Afterall, time was of the essence right now, and not a single moment could be wasted.

Arliaya and Reggie were crunching numbers to calculate the speed needed so that the core would not cause the bomb to explode prematurely due to the core's excessive heat. They were also utilizing the cooling system technology from a Volan to help keep the bomb cool.

"It's so amazing how we already have everything we need. There would not be time to try to invent anything new right now," Reggie said, glad that at least this aspect was going relatively smoothly.

"Yes, it appears that the Creator already had made a way for us so that we could succeed."

Soon the transport Volans were ready to go with their crews. Fortius and Thorn loaded up and were on their way.

The Counsel were in prayer to the Creator for help during this process. After the feast, the Counsel entered into a time of fasting, seeking the completion of His will in this endeavor.

Back on Earth, Mr. Conroy was starting up another summit to talk with the World leaders.

"Good evening, everyone. Thank you for joining us again. I'm sure that you are apprised of what is going on. I can see your questions coming across the screen. Yes, we are sending a nuclear bomb to the sun. Yes, we do believe this will work, and we are taking measures to ensure the bomb is transported safely.

There are ships headed this way now to pick everything up. Our team here is working in shifts non-stop. I know these are unsettling times, but rest assured that we are totally committed to this endeavor." He talked more with the leaders giving them information and answering questions.

Before long, the Volans had arrived, and the teams from both planets went to work getting everything together.

Mr. Conroy approached Thorn. "Thorn, how are you doing?"

"The best I can at the time, I reckon. How about you? I know we're chasing fires, but you're here putting them out. Not to mention you are having to deal with all the politicians and red tape."

"All in a day's work. Were you able to rest at all on your trip back?"

"Yes, sir, I did. I could go for a cup of coffee, though. If you have time to join me, I'd like to run something by you."

"Of course!"

As they walked towards the breakroom they continued to talk.

"Mr. Conroy, I do not know how this is going to turn out. I think we're going to succeed. I've just got something sitting in my soul that is prompting this conversation."

"Okay, Thorn. What is it?"

"Well, if I for some reason don't make it back. I would like to ask a favor. I would like my assistant to have my position, and I would like for you to give him this. It's the admin login to my account. I'd like for him to run the account for me."

After a brief pause Mr. Conroy answered. "Thorn, I hope with everything in me that you return fine. I know there are risks in this–I would be naive to think that something couldn't go wrong.

If you have that kind of confidence in him, then that's good enough for me. I'll do just as you've asked."

"Thank you, sir. I really appreciate that. Well, I better drink this coffee while I'm walking. We ain't got time to stand around."

With that they headed back to the cargo bay. As the last of everything was getting loaded up, everyone said their goodbyes and were off to the sun.

Arliaya and Reggie had finished up all the calculations, and now they just had to wait for the others to return. They took this opportunity to just chat. They talked about many things. The longer they talked the closer they felt to each other. It sounded crazy to them both. They were from different worlds and now was not the time for such things. Or was it?

Finally, Reggie mustered up the nerve to express how he was feeling. "Arliaya, I don't mean to be forward, but I have to tell you. You are the most beautiful sight I have ever seen. I have now seen two worlds and the magnificent sights that they offer. From the sunrise over the gulf to this beautiful sky that you have here. They all pale in comparison to your beauty." He paused, trying to analyze Arliaya's surprised face. "Then there is your intelligence and intriguing character. I know we've only known each other for a very short time, but I really, really like you. I know this isn't the best timing, but I had to tell you."

By the end of his speech, Arliaya had a smile that she was trying to hide. She carefully answered, "Thank you for those beautiful words. I have never had someone speak to me like that. I have also never had someone whose company I enjoy so much as yours. I share your feelings as well. I wish I could say more, but I'm really at a loss for words at this point."

"I'm so very glad to hear that. I was really hoping that I didn't offend you." Reggie was relieved and ecstatic at her answer.

"Not at all. On the contrary, I'm very flattered."

"All I can say is that I really hope this works. Because I've just met you, and I really would like to get to know you more."

"Going to be tough with you on Earth and me here."

"Well, about that, uh, I've decided I'm not going back. You see y'all need help here with getting everything converted over. With it being technology that I am familiar with and even some I developed. I thought it best that I stay. I've already communicated this to my team on Earth."

"No ulterior motives there huh?" Arliaya said with a mischievous grin.

"Maybe," Reggie admitted with a slight blush creeping up in his cheeks.

Just then they heard the announcement that the transports were close and would be landing soon. So up they got and waited for the landing.

As soon as they landed the work began. As soon as they unloaded everything, they began to merge the boring machine with the Volan. Once again, it was amazing how well the technology went together. It was as though the two parts were made for this.

They had to connect the Game Changer near the rear of the vessel. As this was all happening, they began to go over the plan.

Reggie began by pointing at a drawing board that they had been writing information down on.

"This is the speed at which the vessel will have to go so that everything goes as planned. Much slower than this and the bomb may go off prematurely. The... what are we calling this thing? The Volan Digger?"

Everyone kinda nodded their heads in agreement.

"Okay, then, the Volan Digger will discharge to the rear what it is boring through on the front end. This will form a barrier that will stop any back blast from the bomb. Once it reaches this point," he pointed to the designs on the board, "we will have to engage the bomb. This will speed up the entire thing forcing it into the core. Thus, re-energizing the core and voila."

"Looks good, Doc." Thorn replied back.

"Yes, now we just need a command center where we can remote control everything, so it runs like clockwork."

Thorn and Fortius just looked at each other with a grim face and then back at Reggie.

Thorn then said, "Doc, we're not going to remote it. There's going to be too much dirt that could block the signal, and it's not a chance that we can afford to take. After all, we've only got one shot at this."

"What do you mean, not going to remote it? I mean how else are you planning on...."

Then it hit Reggie that they were planning on manning the Volan Digger. His emotions began to get a hold of him.

"No, No, No, No, there has got to be another way. I can design a remote that will work. I just need.."

Thorn interrupted, "Time, Doc, and we don't have much of that. Even if you did make it. We wouldn't be able to test run it. It's too much of a risk. We're going to have to drive it."

With a tremble in his voice Reggie asked, "Who is going to man it?"

Thorn placing his hand on Reggie's shoulder said, "Fortius and I are. It's going to take two men to run it. Plus, you need a second man just in case something goes wrong. That way there is still someone to man it."

Reggie, overcome with tears at this point, fell on Thorns shoulder and embraced him.

"Thorn this is a suicide mission."

"No, Doc, this is a salvation mission. We are making the sacrifice to save two worlds. This Doc, this is exactly what Jesus would do."

Arliaya grabbed Fortius by the hand and started to speak when he stopped her.

"Arliaya, I've got to do this. If I had listened sooner, we may have not been in this position. It's largely my fault, so I have to fix it."

With tears streaming down her face, she hugged Fortius.

"You are a great man, Fortius." Then turning to Thorn, she said, "You both are."

After a few minutes everyone did the best, they could to pull themselves together. As the task still lay ahead of them. The crews worked throughout the night preparing all the machinery to spec.

Finally, it was time.

Reggie grabbed Thorns hand in a firm handshake. "Thorn, it has been my absolute pleasure knowing you. You are the greatest example I have ever met. I," as he began to choke back the tears, "I am going to miss you, my friend."

Thorn just smiled really big and pulled Reggie in giving him a great big bear hug. He leant in and told Reggie, "Lean on Jesus, He can help you heal."

Thorn then released Reggie and turned to Fortius and said, "Well my new, old friend are you ready?"

Fortius replied, "As ready as I'll ever be."

With that, Thorn and Fortius loaded into the Volan Digger. They took one of the cameras with them. They knew they would lose signal eventually but would broadcast as long as they were able to. They would also be communicating from the vessel, but again, they would lose signal eventually. There would come a point after signal loss that everyone would just have to sit and wait. The only way to know if it worked is if the Columns would begin to heat up. So, there were teams stationed at different Columns so they could radio back if anything changed.

Contact was established with Zindwhich and the vessel so everyone could listen in.

Arliaya called out. "Everyone ready? And go in 3, 2, 1 engage."

The Volan Digger fired up and was off digging away. Thorn and Fortius kept reporting back that everything was fine, and the trajectory was on point. They were using an internal guiding system that detected the heat of the core as a compass. Although things were going just as planned, everyone was on the edge of their seats.

After a while, the signal started getting a little spotty. They would catch words here and there until finally nothing. Then the wait began. The silence was deafening in the command center. They paced back and forth hoping to know soon. It seemed like years had passed. Arliaya and Reggie stood at the door of the command center looking into the distance at the Columns. This was their only communication now. All of a sudden, the Columns began to glow brightly, the teams stationed all began to call back at the same time overlapping each other. They were reporting that the Columns were heating back up. Cheers erupted on both worlds as everyone hugged and shook hands in victory. Soon thereafter, the Exterius of the sun was back to normal.

Reggie and Arliaya looked at each other and in unison said, "IT WORKED!" as they held each other tightly. Tears ran down their faces as the bittersweetness set in. While it did work, they lost their friends in the process.

Celebration feasts broke out on both worlds. It was a time of unity. The grave danger had passed and at last everyone was safe.

Reggie turns to Arliaya and says, "I'm so very glad that this worked and that y'all contacted us."

Arliaya responded "Me, too. We would have contacted Venus, but honestly they don't have the technology."

"WAIT! WHAT?"

Back on Earth, Mr. Conroy met with Thorn's assistant and honored his agreement with Thorn. With a feeling of appreciation and love, the assistant signed onto the account for the very first time of many.

"Hello there, you may not know me, but Thorn was my mentor and my friend. My name is Mason. I am a direct product of mercy and grace. I am here to tell you what Jesus would do.

Part 2

Frozen In Time

Frozen in Time Chapter 1

A few years passed by since the crew at Zindwhich industries teamed up with the Zaya people, saved the sun and, subsequently, the Earth. There were new faces around the facility. Dr. Lea Swanson had filled Reggie's position as one of the lead scientists at the facility. She also happened to be the twin sister to Mason that had filled Thorns position. They enjoyed working together. As siblings, though, they were a little different with each other than they were with others.

"Hey Lea, there is something strange going on." Mason said as he approached Lea. "The weather forecast changed."

"Mason, that's not strange, the forecast always changes. Honestly, I should have been a meteorologist. I could be wrong half the time, and nobody would even question it."

"No, not like that. I'm talking about.."

"The lightning storms. Yes, that is admittedly strange. These random lightning storms, if you want to call them that, keep popping up. The funny thing is..."

Mason stepped in slightly frustrated at being interrupted, "I'm not talking about the lightning storms. I'm talking about this newspaper."

"Oh, because a newspaper is more interesting than a lightning storm. Tell me, Mason, did your newspaper turn the television on for you this morning and take out the trash?"

"Come on, Lea, I'm serious."

"Seriously funny. I'm not falling for one of your pranks, and I'm really trying to figure out this random lightning."

"LEA!" he exclaimed, as he grabbed her by the hand, "I'm really serious. I'm not playing."

"Okay, okay. I'm sorry. In my defense you are apt to pull a prank. You have my attention."

"So, this newspaper, I had it at home. Yesterday, the forecast called for clear skies this weekend. Now though it's calling for rain."

"Whoa, whoa, whoa, little brother. You're trying to tell me that the newspaper at your house just randomly changed?" She stared at him for a moment and burst into laughter. "I knew you were messing with me. Good one, Mason, but I've gotta get back to work."

"Lea, I'm not kidding, and you're only a minute and a half older than me." Though Mason loved his sister, he hated that she liked to use the "I'm older card" on him when it was only such a short difference in time.

"That's older."

"Anyway," Mason decided not to argue, "It's not just the weather. Yesterday, the article on this page was a story about the zoo and its new exhibit. Now it's about the new restaurant that just opened across town."

"Look, I played your game, but I really do have work to do. Tell you what, I have the same newspaper over here on my desk. I'll just grab it. See it's -she paused for a second- it's different." She looked intently at the paper and then up at Mason. "Oh, you almost got me. You had a different newspaper printed just to mess with me didn't you. I gotta admit that's a good one, even for you."

Lea began laughing again as she shook her head and went back to work.

"I give up." Mason said as he tossed the newspaper in the trash and walked out.

Lea went back to her research. These lightning storms, as she had mentioned earlier, were not really storms. There was no thunder, no rain, and no warning on any radar. They just appeared randomly and only lasted minutes. Plus, they were happening all within a half mile radius from Zindwhich.

She had begun to wonder if all the travels to and from the sun had left a lingering effect at the facility. Not only were there the trips when they were trying to save the sun, but once or twice a year Reggie would return to visit. Not to mention he had taken a few people to the sun, including Mr. Conroy and the General. She was not certain, but it was the only thing that she could think of that would make Zindwhich different than any other place. She decided to consult one of her colleagues, Dr. Ernest Franklin. She could have contacted Reggie, but she felt like it was a trivial matter to bother him with seeing as he was now one of the heads of an intergalactic counsel, but we'll get into that later.

Dr. Ernest Franklin Jr. had been with Zindwhich for some time. He, like Lea, was a scientist. He was a very intelligent man, but he was also a little eccentric and quirky. Nobody thought much of it just because sometimes intelligent people are that way. He always had a head full of grayish silver, frazzled hair. Though most of the employees at Zindwhich dressed informally, he always had his long, white lab coat on with his slacks and black framed glasses. He was the walking picture of a scientist. Often people would pick that he was the "mad scientist" of the facility. He worked the majority of the time by himself. He did work for Zindwhich during the sun burnout event, but he never got involved with it. He preferred to continue working on his projects.

He and Lea did work on a few projects together though and enjoyed each other's company. He was like an uncle to Lea, so much so that she actually grew to call him Uncle Ernie. He would correct most people if they called him Ernie with a firm "Its Ernest" comment, but not Lea. He too saw her like family. One thing he never spoke of, however, was his own family. Even if prodded, he would not so subtly change the subject.

Randomly, Lea enjoyed swinging by his office to bring him cupcakes and coffee. Or with whatever snack happened to be in the breakroom. This being said, her stopping by this day was no new or surprising thing. She entered his lab and shouted out, "Uncle Ernie, where are you at?"

Thump, she heard followed by a groan of, "My head. Why must people shout when they come in? Don't they know I'm busy? I could have had explosives in my hand." He quickly slipped into a tangent talking to himself. "What if I did have explosives in my hands? I could have dropped them and blown up the facility. Then all my research would be gone and my lab. I would be out of a job.."

Lea commented, "And dead!"

"Yes, yes my dear. That too. It would be most unfortunate. Oh, cupcakes and coffee thank you. What brought you by today?"

"The weather."

"Yes, the weather. Umm, I'm sorry dear, I for the life of me can't remember what it was we were saying about the weather."

Not worrying about the fact, they hadn't yet begun the conversation, Lea simply jumped into the situation at hand. "It's the lightning Uncle Ernie, it's coming and going sporadically. It only lasts for a couple minutes and it's always close to Zindwhich."

"Really?" He said with a mouthful of cupcake. "Hold on dear, I must, hold on," as he choked down the piece of cupcake with coffee. "Sorry about that," he apologized once he was able to speak clearly. "I have not noticed. When did it start?"

"A couple of weeks ago. I'm wondering if it has something to do with Zindwhich being the hub for going and coming from the sun, if there isn't a lingering effect from that? I know it sounds far-fetched."

"We are scientists dear; we are supposed to reach for the far-fetched. We are to stretch our imaginations to its very limits to find the answers that others are not willing to reach for."

"I love how you put things. It makes so much more sense when you say it."

"Thank you my dear. Now about this lightning, tell me more."

They talked for some time about the lightning storms and how they may or may not correlate to sun travel. They were deep in conversation when Mason began to approach the lab doors.

Mason was quite the prankster and thoroughly loved startling Ernest. He, with his phone in hand, was doing a live video on Thorns old website. He quietly said, "This is probably not what Jesus would do, but who knows. I mean scripture says that laughter doeth good like a medicine, right?" With that he slammed the doors open WHAMM, the doors went as he burst in and yelled "AGGHH!"

Ernest let out a shout of fear that could have sounded like a cat with its tail caught in a meat grinder.

Meanwhile, Mason was lying on the floor in tears, laughing so hard he could hardly breathe.

Lea, who was also startled by this, shouted, "MASON, you're going to give someone a heart attack one day!"

Mason, continuing to laugh and try to regain his composure, said in between laughing, "Hey, Sis, I'm just making sure y'all's hearts are working right. I'm giving them good exercise so they can stand the pressure later. I mean, y'all do it all the time right, test things beyond the pressure that they are meant to stand?"

Ernest spoke up. "Mr. Mason, though I can appreciate your comparison, that is not at all how it works. I swear if I were not a gentle man, I'd strap you to a rocket and fly you into the heart of Venus."

"Whoa, Doc, calm down. I'm just playing man. Don't be get any crazy ideas." He said, holding his free hand up in mock surrender as he was still laughing. "I'll leave you two alone to do your work. I just wanted to bring your shipment to you. You asked me to bring it as soon as it arrived."

With that, Ernest forgot everything else that was going on. "Yes, yes, my good man. Thank you! I really must get back to work. Excuse me, will you?" He said as he walked away.

Mason looked at Lea and said, "I'd say that's weird, but look who I'd be talking about." He began to chuckle again as he walked away.

Lea says to herself, "Well, I guess it's back to the drawing board."

Time seemed to fly over the next few hours, and the day was winding down.

Mason went to Lea's lab and asked, "Hey, sis, you wanna try out the new restaurant across town? My treat."

"Please tell me that this isn't you still trying to pull a prank on me. You just mentioned that restaurant from your magical newspaper this morning."

"Look, you can believe me or not, but I was telling the truth about the paper. As far as the restaurant goes, I just thought we could go eat. It looks good so whatcha say, sis?"

"Okay fine, but I swear if this is a prank..."

"I know, you'll strap me to a rocket and fly me into the heart of Venus," Mason said with an exasperated laugh. Although even he had to admit it did sound a little crazy.

"No. I was going to say, I'm going to punch you in the face."

"That scares me more than Venus. Let's go." Mason started to walk out when he added, "Oh and, by the way, I don't think punching me in the face is what Jesus would do."

"I don't know sometimes with you." She said with a giggle. Lea was happy to see Mason had truly turn his life around. She would always be in debt to the man that helped him turn his life around. She didn't get to spend much time with Thorn herself, but she knew the world lost a special man when he died.

As they were about to pull out the gate Mason leaned out the window and spoke to the security guard. "Hey Al, how old are the boys now?"

Al responded beaming with pride, "Almost four years old now." His love for his boys was always very evident when the spoke of them.

"Here," Mason said, "give them these," as he handed him a baseball, bat, and gloves. "Tell them Jesus loves them for me."

"Thanks, Mason, I sure will."

"Well," says Leah, "you can be nice."

"Hey, I'm always nice!"

"Hmmph." Lea rolled her eyes so hard Mason was almost worried they would get stuck.

As they made it to the restaurant, they went to the rooftop view to dine. They were chatting over things and enjoying their meal. All of a sudden, another lightning storm hit, bigger than the previous ones, but still it only lasted minutes.

"I've got to figure this out," said Lea, equally frustrated and inquisitive. "When we're done would you mind running me back to work?"

"I mean, I will, but you've gotta rest sometime."

"Says the night owl."

"Yeah, yeah, yeah, I hear you."

Once they finished, they went back to work as Lea requested. While they were still on their way, another series of lightning shot off, but again stopped quickly.

Mason even commented, "That is kinda weird."

As they were pulling in, they saw Ernest walking out of the building in a rush. They tried to wave him down, but he was too focused on where he was going.

Lea arrived at her lab and fired up some of her machinery that could measure the lightning and the residual effects in the air. She had not been able to take any measurements close to the time that any of the lightning happened as of yet, so this was a great opportunity. As she got everything going, the machine was making a whirring sound. Information began to pop up on her computer. She began shaking her head as she read it over. After a few moments, she began to talk to Mason.

"This doesn't make sense."

"What's that, Sis?"

"Well, according to this, the lightning is actually coming from here. Like something here is generating it." She paused, not quite understanding how this could be possible. "Something here is making the lightning, but what?"

"Lea, I think you need to contact Reggie."

Frozen in Time Chapter 2

Now Reggie had been a very busy person. Since his time living on the sun, he and Arliaya had revolutionized how they produced power. With the knowledge of life on other planets, he headed up a team of scientists, elders, and other leaders to share knowledge across the galaxy. He and Arliaya traveled to different planets giving conferences and setting up schools so that everyone could learn. Not to mention that He and Arliaya had gotten married and had a set of twin boys, Case Elijah, and Justin Elisha. They honeymooned in Galveston, after the wedding, where Arliaya got to experience her first sunrise over the gulf.

They had also upgraded the communication system between Zindwhich and the sun so that it was easier to communicate and added their own devices so that they could be reached by either planet in case they were needed. They were in the process of having this done throughout the galaxy. This did make it much easier for Lea to contact them. They were wrapping up a conference when they received the call.

Arliaya answered the call.

"Hello."

"Hello, Mrs. Arliaya, this is Lea, from earth."

"Yes, Lea, so nice to hear from you. How are things with you?"

"Oh, I am well. How are the twins?"

"They are something else to say the least. Too smart for their age. I think they'll likely surpass Reggie and I one day."

"That they may. Is Reggie there? I was actually wanting to speak to him?"

"He will be here shortly. I am currently in our personal Volan with the boys. We had just finished a conference, so I loaded the boys up. I think he'll be here. Wait a minute, here he comes now."

Reggie entered the Volan. "That was a good conference. Don't you think, my love?"

"Yes, love, here Lea is on the radio."

"Lea from earth?"

"Do we know another one?"

"No, I guess not. I'm sorry, silly question."

"Lea, Reggie here, how are you?"

"I am well, sir. I have an issue here that I can't seem to figure out, however. I was wondering if I could get you to help me look into it?"

Reggie looked at Arliaya, who nodded her head yes. "Well, I'm always up for a challenge and you're in luck. We are actually free for a few days. We'll head that way."

"Amazing, thank you, thank you, thank you."

"You are very welcome. We'll see you soon."

While they waited for their arrival, Lea and Mason decided to go home for the night and rest.

Reggie and his family arrived early the next morning before people had started showing up for the workday– only the night guards were there– so they went to Reggie's condo first to settle in. As they were unpacking, Reggie stopped and noticed that the building was a different color. He wondered when it had been painted and honestly why the building manager hadn't contacted him about changing the color. He didn't think much else of it, however, as he was helping Arliaya with the boys.

Arliaya told Reggie, "You know I would love to go with you, but the boys need to unwind. I'm going to take them to the beach and let them play."

"That sounds like a wonderful idea. I'll be back later."

As he was walking out, he spotted the building manager. "Hey, Ralph, hey how have you been?"

"I'm good Reggie, and yourself? What brings you to town?"

"Some of the folks at Zindwhich wanted me to swing by, so here I am. Hey, just curious when did you get the buildings painted? Not that I mind, it looks good."

"I honestly don't know what you are talking about, Reggie. They've always been this color. I mean as long as you and I have been here."

Reggie pierced his lips a little and with a squint in his eye said, "I don't recall them being this color. Well, maybe I've just been traveling too much, and it's got me messed up. Oh well, nice to see you again, Ralph."

"You too, Reggie."

With that he was off to Zindwhich. As he arrived it took him a little time to get in the building as he was catching up with everyone as he ran into them. Finally, he made it inside and spotted Mason.

"Hey there, young man. How are you?"

"Mr. Reggie! Hey, it's so good to see you. It has been a while."

"Yes, it has. I've been following your website. You know, Thorn would be proud."

As he dropped his head a little with a smile he said, "Thank you, Mr. Reggie. That means a lot to me. I sure do miss him. I go back and watch his videos quite often. I want to be like him so much and run his website the way he would. I just, I don't know how."

"I miss him too. He was a dear friend to me. I will tell you this, though. He used to say, "If you spend all your time trying to be somebody else, then there ain't no time left to be yourself." So, you run the website like you would. I'm sure if he were here, he'd probably tell you not to worry about being like him but be like Jesus."

"That does sound like something that he would say."

"Yep, but hey. If you don't stop scaring Ernest, you're going to be joining Thorn."

"You saw that? That was hilarious. Man, I got him so good and Lea. Oh she's going to want to see you. I'll walk with you."

As they arrived in the lab, Lea was already there busy trying to figure this out.

"I remember those days," said Reggie.

"Hey, Mr. Reggie. It's so good to see you. Thank you for coming. Where is Mrs. Arliaya and the twins?"

"She thought it best to let them play for a while."

"She's probably right." Lea agreed. "I want to go ahead and show you, my problem. You see, we've been having these lightning storms. Honestly, I've started calling them occurrences. Because they aren't really storms. They originate from here at Zindwhich. Originally, I was thinking that because the travel from the sun to earth mostly comes through here, and that maybe that was the cause. I'm really not sure, but by my readings last night it's being generated from here."

"Well, let's have a look."

As they ran over data and such it kept looking like it really didn't have much to do with the travel. It was more likely something going on there. It was also too sporadic. They began to try to nail down the problem. As the day went on Reggie decided to go to lunch with his family.

As he was walking out, he noticed the newspaper that Mason had brought in still on the top of the trash can. He picked it up to browse over it. He asked Lea, "Is this restaurant a good place to eat?"

Lea responded, "Yes sir, we ate there last night. I thought Mason took that thing with him. He was talking about how the newspaper had somehow magically changed overnight. He even had that fake paper printed so it would be different than the one I had."

This actually caught Reggie's attention because he remembered the color change of the buildings. He tucked it away and went to lunch. While at lunch he kept noticing subtle differences throughout the city. This was becoming more puzzling. He finished his lunch and called Lea.

"Lea, I'm noticing differences throughout town. I'm not talking about just the colors of buildings and such. I'm talking about roadways being different. Stores that were once here, gone."

"I'm sorry, Reggie, I'm not sure what you are talking about.

"Something is awry. I'm on my way back."

Arliaya took the twins back to the condo for a nap and planned to go into Zindwhich later.

As Reggie arrived his brain was stirring as he started talking to Lea. "Okay, so somehow things around town are changing. Funny thing is nobody notices it. The newspaper from yesterday. I don't think it was a trick. I think it was an anomaly."

"What do you mean?"

"Well, it appears that if something is at Zindwhich, it stays the same. Or it does for a while, not sure how long. If though, it's not here, it changes. Just like the newspaper that Mason had. You see he left it at his apartment. Your paper however was left here. It's also affecting people's memories. Things are changing and people don't even know that they have. To them it's like it has always been that way. Whatever is happening is kinda like a ripple effect in water. When something disturbs water, the ripples go outward. The wider they go out the less you feel them. Now for some reason the effects aren't being felt here immediately. I'm not sure how long that will last. Somehow the lightning is changing things or whatever is causing the lightning is. I believe that because I was not on earth, it didn't affect me. I still remember the way things were. We definitely have to figure this out and fix it as soon as possible."

"Well, umm, I don't know what to say. I'm glad I called you."

"Yes, let's get to work."

They worked tirelessly running numbers. As it neared evening and everyone was leaving for the day, they had gotten no closer to an answer. They decided to go talk to Ernest and see if maybe he could help. Mason joined them on the way down. As they neared his lab everything started flashing. Like a disco ball, a kaleidoscope and a strobe light were all dancing around the room together. Then there was a bright flash. They rushed in only to find nothing, but a little smoke settling in the very back of the lab.

They began to call out all at once "Ernest, Uncle Ernie, Dr. Franklin, Hello."

Nothing, there was nothing. Then Lea got a notification that a lightning storm had just happened.

She tells Reggie, "Whatever just happened down here triggered a lightning storm."

"What has he been working on?"

"I honestly don't know. There was a stack of things here in the back, but I thought they were just junked ideas."

A few minutes passed as they were discussing the situation. When the flashing lights began again. Although there was no source of wind in the room other than air conditioning, the wind began to blow around them. They took cover not knowing what was happening. Soon a vessel appeared out of nowhere. It was somewhat shaped like an Erlenmeyer flask. It had a large flat bottom base, a conical body, and a tube-shaped neck at the top. The door opened and what looked like a fog rolled out onto the floor. Then Ernest emerged from the vessel talking to himself, in what sounded like nonsense.

"No, that wasn't right. That was only ten. I need more, but how? I gotta find a way to. Maybe I could. No, that wouldn't work. I..."

"Ernest!" Exclaimed Reggie. "What in the world are you doing?"

Ernest let out a yell, then said: "Oh my lands. You scared me. Why must people always scare me? I didn't think anyone was here."

"Ernest, I'm going to repeat, what are you doing? What are you working on? What's with the disappearing act? Is this a teleportation machine?"

"Well, you see. Well, I uhh. I, I didn't know anyone was here. Umm."

"Spit it out, man."

"Well, it's not a teleportation machine. Though that would be interesting," he said as began to wander off in thought, "with a few adjustments I probably could. Yes, I think I could possibly make that work. I'll draw it out, yes. I'll do that."

Lea gently grabbed Ernest by the arm. "Uncle Ernie, what is this machine, and what are you doing with it?"

"Oh, yes, my dear, I'm sorry I got distracted again. It's a little hard to explain, but I guess we are all scientists and Reggie, you have traveled to the sun. Oh, my goodness, Reggie! How are you, my friend? It has been ages since I saw you last. We must have a chat over coffee, coffee, yes I need coffee."

Lea gently nudged, "Focus."

"Oh, yes. It's a time machine."

Frozen in Time Chapter 3

"A TIME MACHINE?" Reggie exclaimed. "Ernest, do you know the ramifications of traveling through time? I mean it's impressive, yes, but the space-time continuum! You cannot travel through time without causing changes. RIPPLES!!! That's what is causing the changes and the ripple changes are actually butterfly effect. Ernest, do you know what you're doing?"

"I'm traveling through time."

"No, I mean do you know what you're doing to everything else? You are changing things, and if you don't stop it's going to get worse."

"I didn't mean to cause any harm. I had calculated for that. You see this machine here. I call it the butterfly net. I designed it to prevent any butterfly effects. It would catch them so to speak and work kind of like autocorrect does when you are typing. I guess I didn't have it calibrated correctly. I really thought I had calculated everything."

"Well, that does explain why the building and its contents don't change."

Lea asks, "What were you trying to accomplish?"

Ernest looked at her with a steely focus, "I have two reasons and two only for this time machine. One is that I need to correct some past mistakes I've made."

Mason spoke up, "Ernest, we've all made mistakes. I mean I've really made my share, but you have to learn to live with them and learn from them. You can't change the past."

"Those are wise words my boy, but I can change the past. Once I get the machine working correctly."

"But you don't need to. I mean you're causing mistakes now."

"Yes, I understand that. I believe I can fix that too, with the right technology."

"Look, it's not like you killed anybody."

"Well, son, I may not have killed them myself, but I am responsible."

"You can't blame yourself for accidents."

Ernest lowered his head for a moment. He then looked at them intently, "You all might want to sit down. I've hidden this too long, so please listen and don't stop me for questions. You see I'm not actually what you would call an earthling. I'm from Venus."

A look of bewilderment came over their faces.

"I've lived here on Earth for a very long time. It started so many years ago that I don't even remember how long ago it was. I lived on Venus, and I was always trying to invent things. Unfortunately, the technology on Venus is lacking. One day, by chance or by divine appointment, a traveler from the sun crash landed on Venus. He was having trouble with his transportation vehicle. I assisted him in getting it back up and running, and I also pointed out some design flaws. After some conversation he agreed to take me to the sun with him. I assured him that I could help him with his design, given the right technology. Soon, we arrived on the sun. We redesigned the vessel so that it could travel faster than before and easily go through the Exterius of the sun."

Reggie spoke up, "You designed the Volan?"

Ernest just looked at him.

"Sorry, I forgot. I'll wait."

Ernest continued, "Yes, I helped design the Volans. I also helped design and build their power grid, including the blankets that were placed on the Columns that absorbed the heat. I did not take into account what harm they may cause. My friend and I would travel the galaxy. Earth was always my favorite place to visit. I took a liking to Galveston. On one particular visit, I met the most beautiful being that I have ever seen in my life. I enjoyed being with her so much that I convinced my friend to let me stay. He checked on me randomly, and we kept in touch with a radio system that I designed. It's the same technology that I used to design the radio system here at Zindwhich years later."

Reggie started to speak, but quickly stopped when Ernest glanced his way again.

"I spent all the time I could with the woman that I had met. Eventually we married, and I settled into life on Earth, happily blending in. I got a job. We had a beautiful little girl. She was my pride and joy. My greatest creation! There was a problem, though. The people from Venus live much longer than the people from earth. We actually live longer than those from the sun as well, but I digress. So, I knew that I would outlive my wife, though old age ended up not being the thing to take her from me. Sometime after she was gone, I faked my death. You see, I could not just stay around, and nobody suspect anything when I didn't die, or age, like anyone else. This way my daughter, Adeline who was 35 at the time, could live a normal life and not have to deal with the issues that would arise. I changed my name and continued to live my life. I guess I could have left earth and gone to another planet, but this is where the love of my life was. Even though she was not alive anymore, this was her home, this was our home. So, I changed my name. I moved to another part of town, but for the same reason that I couldn't leave earth, I couldn't leave Galveston. I blended into the crowd. I always kept watch over my daughter. Although she never knew it. You learn to be sneaky when you've been around as long as I have. Anyway, I lived an entire life over, though I was able to keep my name this time by becoming a junior. This did make things easier. Plus, I can leave everything to myself in a will, so I don't have to start over. Well, one day, my old friend contacted me. There was a problem with the sun, it was going out. I directed him to contact Zindwhich, I knew that they would eventually reach you, Reggie. I knew that you could figure it all out. You are one of the most intelligent beings that I have ever met. We all know how things worked out. Though, it mostly worked out for the good. There was a flaw. My original design on the sun caused the death of my dear friends Fortius, the one that brought me to earth and Thorn, who befriended me here. Thorn was a special man and was very dear to me. I lost two friends because of something that I had done, and I needed to fix that. So, I started designing the time machine." Ernest stopped and looked at those in front of him. "So, there you have it." He continued when they said nothing.

All three of them stood there for a second, almost in shock.

Finally, Reggie spoke. "Ernest, that is a lot to take in. You knew Fortius? Wow! And you designed the Volans. That, that is amazing, but Ernest, you can't blame yourself for all of this. Thorn and Fortius made a choice. It was theirs to make. Yes, you may have made the original design on the sun, but what's done is done. You can't unring a bell."

Mason chimed in, "Ernest, you know what Thorn meant to me, but I agree with Mr. Reggie. You can't blame yourself for this."

Ernest looked at Mason and said, "You don't blame me for the loss of your friend?"

"No sir, and in case you need to hear it, I forgive you."

A tear ran down his face, "Thank you Mason, for that. I cannot tell you what that means to me."

"That's what Jesus would do."

"Yes, I guess it is."

Lea, who had been quiet throughout this stepped in and said, "So, I've got questions. How are you able to stand the temperature here? Venus is incredibly hot."

"Well child, Venus is similar to the sun in make-up. What you see is an outer core temperature. Though the inside is still hot, it is not near the temperature of the outside. The other thing is that people from Venus, well, we can stand extreme temperatures in both directions. From cold to hot."

"Okay. What about your other reason? You said there were two reasons."

"My wife, I've loved one woman in all my years. I lost her in 1961 when Hurricane Carla hit Galveston. Our daughter and I had made it to a bunker that I had built. She was caught across town and never made it. She was 58, and I never even got to tell her goodbye."

"Well, now, I'm crying. That's a beautiful sentiment. What was her name?"

"Martha Lea Lowman."

Lea and Mason looked at each other seriously then back at Ernest.

"That's our great grandmother's name. Are you telling us that you are...?"

"Ernest Mason Lowman is the name that I went by then. Yes, I'm your great grandfather."

They both just stared at him, not knowing what to say or how to feel.

Finally, Reggie broke the silence. "Well, why don't you two give your great grandfather a hug. I'm sure he's gone too many years without one."

They both embraced him tightly. He held them close, and it seemed for the first time in decades he felt love.

"Well, guys, I hate to break up a family reunion, but there is still the problem of the time machine."

Ernest responded, "Yes, I think I can use the technology from a Volan and fix what is missing and undo what I have done."

"You're still wanting to go back?"

"I'm sorry, Reggie, I should have been more clear. I can go back and undo the more recent things done. Putting things back in their right order."

"Ah, gotcha. Well, would you like some help?"

"Yes, I think I would. Mason, would you mind retrieving the Volan from up top while we begin work down here?"

"Sure thing, Gramps," Mason replied with a smile.

Ernest just looked at him with squinted eyes and a half grin.

Lea said, "I think that is the first time I've seen you smile."

"Yes, it has been a long time."

As they begin working on the time machine, Mason went upstairs to get the Volan. Lea went with him to grab cupcakes and coffee for everyone from the breakroom.

"Wow, our great grandfather," she said.

"I know right. That's crazy."

"Man, I can't wait to tell mom about this."

"Yeah right. What about Grammy? I mean I know she's in a nursing home but that's her dad."

"You're right. That is going to be so amazing."

As they exited the elevator, they immediately noticed something was wrong. Lea rushed to the intercom and called downstairs.

"You guys might want to get up here. Now!"

Reggie and Ernest with a look of confusion stopped what they were doing and headed upstairs. As they made it to the lobby they were floored. Everything outside the building was frozen completely.

Ernest exclaimed, "How did this happen? It was just 80 degrees. I don't understand."

Reggie asked, "How far did you say you went back last time?"

"I made it ten years back, why?"

"You changed the timeline. Arliaya was the one that had discovered the issues on the sun and brought them to the attention of Fortius. Without her the sun would have gone out."

"Okay, what does that have to do with this?"

"She was here on Earth at the condo with my children. You erased her out of the last ten years of existence and consequently my children. Hence she was not on the sun to warn anyone and now the Earth is frozen, and the sun is gone." Reggie said with a hint of anger in his voice, as he had just lost his family.

"OH, NO! I'm so sorry, Reggie! I never meant for this to happen."

Reggie took a deep breath and calmed himself down. "Ernest, we can fix this. That is the only reason I'm not losing it right now. We will continue to work on the time machine. We will reset the timeline and fix everything. Now let's get to work."

Frozen in Time Chapter 4

Mason, "Why are we not frozen? Why is the building not frozen when everything around it is?"

Lea responds, "Because this is ground zero. It's the ripple effect that Mr. Reggie was talking about. It sends waves out that affect the outside area first. If you look into the distance everything is solid ice. It appears that directly outside of the building is frozen, but it appears to be freshly frozen. So my thought is that right outside isn't as cold as say a mile out."

"Well how long until the building and we along with it freeze?"

"I don't know."

"Well, that's not comforting at all."

Reggie stated "It's not, but it is what it is at this point. As far as we are aware, we are the only four people left in existence. If we are going to turn this around, we've got to work together, and we've got to work fast. As Lea said, we don't know how long we have. First things first, let's get the Volan. Where is it?"

Mason pointed outside across the tarmac to one of the hangers that was frozen along with everything else.

"Great, that's just great. Now we have to figure out how to get across a frozen wasteland, load it up and get it back inside. Then we have to pray that it's not frozen beyond use. What else could go wrong?"

"Whoa Doc, settle down a little. I know things look bad; I mean they look really bad. I know you've just lost everything you hold dear to your heart, but we've gotta trust God. We'll pray and ask for God's help, and we have to trust that He will help. You see Doc, you don't have to trust God when you understand what's going on. No trust is when everything is going wrong, and you still trust God."

Reggie took a deep breath, looked at Mason and said, "You're more like Thorn than you realize, Mason. Thank you, I needed that."

"My pleasure, Doc. Now, let's go to my shop because I've got something there that just might help."

As they begin to walk Lea commended Mason on how he handled the situation. She expressed how proud she was of him for turning his life around and how much of an inspiration he was to her.

Ernest sheepishly begins to try to talk to Reggie.

"Reggie, I'm incredibly sorry for, well for erasing your family. I never meant to. I would never have tried to harm your family. I, I..."

Reggie placed his hand on Ernest's shoulder and responded, "Ernest, I can't blame you. I've only been a few minutes without my wife and children and I'm already ready to do anything to get them back. You have been without your wife for decades. I can only imagine what you've been through, old friend."

"Thank you, thank you for that. Unfortunately, I spent so long mourning her loss that I couldn't enjoy her life or mine. I have two beautiful grandchildren there that I could have been spending more time with. Instead, I was building an infernal time machine that caused more harm than it's worth."

"It's okay Ernest. We will fix this. You weren't trying to hurt anyone. You just missed your wife."

"I do hope you're correct. I was so blind to see that she could have lived on through them. I could have told them sooner. I tried so hard to protect my family. I knew years ago that I wouldn't be accepted if people knew I was from Venus, but now that everyone knows. I could have come out and told my story once Fortius first contacted me. I could have come to you directly. I was just still trying to hide. I wasn't even trying to protect my family at that point. Because if I was trying to protect them, I would have said something. I was, I was just so used to hiding."

"I'm sorry you've had to hide so long. Speaking of that, I have a question just how old are you?"

"Well, I'm not as old as Methuselah, but I'm older than Enoch."

"I apologize, I don't know my Bible that well. Methuselah was 969 years old, right?"

"Yes."

"But how old was Enoch?"

"Enoch was 365 years old."

"YOU'RE OLDER THAN THAT?"

"Yes, though I'm not sure exactly how old. You lose track after time. I'm somewhere in the 400's. It's really not that long when you've lived on three planets."

"Man, the things you must have seen."

"None more beautiful than Martha. You know, Lea reminds me of her a lot. Well, both of them really. She was smart like Lea and mischievous like Mason. She loved to scare me so much. I think it was her favorite hobby. Let me tell you about the first time I saw her."

The two continued to talk as they walked along the way to the shop. They almost forgot the overwhelming problem they faced as they went on about each other's wives and families.

Just as they were about to arrive at the shop, Ernest pipes up, "Oh, I've got to tell you one more thing that you may find interesting before we get there. Did you know the chances of twins being in your family rises exponentially when the mother and father are from two different planets?"

"What?!"

With that they arrived at the shop. Mason had everyone stand at the front while he ran to the back of the shop. Soon, they heard a loud noise blast from the rear of the shop. It sounded like thunder being caged inside of a prison cell roaring to get out. Soon a *vroom, vroom, vroom, pop, pop, bratatat* then *BOOM* a backfire let out. Then the thundering sound settled in like the deep growl like that of a lion. Mason emerged from the back driving a most impressive machine. It looked like a semi-truck merged with a train. It was black with red, yellow, and blue flames running most of its length.

Mason came to a stop and hopped out with a proud smile. "Well, folks, what do you think? I call it Samson."

Reggie was the first to speak, "Mason, that thing is a monster."

"Ain't it though," Mason said excitedly, "but a monster is what we're going to need to get through that weather and back."

"You're absolutely right about that. Do you think it will make it?"

"This thing? Oh yeah. This baby has 12 wheels that are 18 inches wide. Each wheel is also equipped with steering, and it can be all wheel drive with the push of a button. It has a 800-horsepower engine. By the way, that is just 200 above the Detroit DD16 engine, just saying. I've got a communication system in here complete with Bluetooth. I've got cameras mounted in the front and back, exterior and interior, that can feed back to the communication system here. The back also opens up completely to make for easier loading and unloading. I even have proximity sensors right inside the back door. I can turn them on or off depending on what I may need at the time. If I have them on, once a load clears them, the doors will close automatically. Neat right? I just gotta get the electric crane hoist installed right quick. Already got the railing installed, just gotta mount the hoist and wire it up. I'll have that done in a jiffy. Oh, and it also has heated seats." He said with a smile.

"Well, I'm impressed!"

Mason quickly had the hoist and was set to go.

He said, "So the plan is to go get the Volan, hook it up and then pull it into the back of the truck. Bring it back in here and take what we need off of it."

Ernest steps in, "It may need to be thawed out, depending on how cold it is. As your sister was saying earlier, it doesn't seem as cold right outside, but the further you go the colder it will get. I'm not sure how you'll hold up to the temperatures. It may be best if I go."

"I appreciate the thought, gramps..."

"You're going to call me that from now on, aren't you?"

"Yep, anyway I appreciate the thought, but I'm the only one that knows how to run this thing. Don't worry about it. God's got this!"

"I appreciate your faith son, but what if, I mean what, what if you don't make it?"

"Well, first of all, this is what Jesus would do, so it's what I have to do."

A lump formed in Reggie's throat as he remembered Thorn doing the same thing.

"Secondly, you see the cables on that big crane over there? Hook them up to the front of Samson. I'll get the Volan in. If I can't make it from there, tow it back into the building."

"Very well."

"Okay. So y'all see that room over there? We call it the safe room. It has specialized tempered glass. I think it will stand the cold for a bit. Y'all take the remote to the crane in there. You'll be safe there and can see straight out once I open the shop door. Also, you can communicate with me from the system in there and link to the cameras. I'll link my Bluetooth to the truck so we can talk. If you have to tow it in, then here is the remote for the shop door. You can close it from there. I'm going to turn the heat up in here as high as I can to help. So, we've got a plan. Let's do this."

Lea grabbed his hand, "You make it back, you hear me?" as she fought back the tears.

"Hey, somebody's gotta stick around and annoy you."

She gently punched his arm and then hugged him like it might be the last time she ever could. Part of her worried it may be.

After a moment, he said, "Okay let's break this up, ain't going to have me crying and freezing tears to my face."

He loaded up in Samson and began to ease towards the door. They all gathered in the safe room. Once everyone was in position, they opened the door to the shop remotely. As the door opened the wind began to blow into the shop. Although they couldn't actually feel the cold yet, the thought of it chilled them to their bones. Mason began to creep across tarmac. Driving in reverse made it slightly more challenging. He did it this way though because he didn't want to try and turn on the ice, plus the cable was hooked to the front of the truck. As he neared the hangar, he just used the truck to push through the roll up door. He felt it was best to spend as little time outside of the truck as possible. Plus, he wasn't sure if the door would be frozen shut. The door was no match for the brute power of Samson, it pushed straight through it with ease. Now that he was backed in and had gotten Samson in position it was time to hook up the Volan. He neared the back of the truck as the group watched on. The back of the truck opened up and Mason truly felt the cold for the first time.

"OH MAN, THAT IS COLD."

Lea quickly asked, "Are you okay?"

"Yeah, that's just cold. That is the coldest thing I've ever felt. Oh well, no turning back now."

"Be careful please."

"Always." Mason said jokingly.

He went right to work. As he was working you could tell he was slowing down. Finally, the Volan was hooked up and he was heading back to the truck. He was almost moving in slow motion at this point as the cold was taking its toll on him. They began to hear his weakened voice through the comms.

"Yea, though I walk through the valley of the shadow of death, I will fear no evil: for thou art with me; thy rod and thy staff they comfort me. Make thy face to shine upon thy servant: save me for thy mercies' sake."

Suddenly he collapsed.

Lea screamed, "MASON, GET UP, PLEASE GET UP!!!"

Slowly he began to crawl back to his feet and fight his way to the truck. You could hear his voice even fainter than before.

"It is God that girdeth me with strength. My help comes from the Lord, who made heaven and earth. For by thee I have run through a troop; and by my God have I leaped over a wall."

With that he fell forward and pressed the button to pull the Volan in. Once it was in the truck, the doors closed automatically.

Everyone was listening for a peep in the silence. It seemed like an eternity passed when Mason's voice pierced through the stillness,

"I told you God's got this."

Frozen in Time Chapter 5

Mason worked his way up to the front to start driving, although they already had the crane pulling the truck back. He fell into the driver's seat and turned the heater vents towards him. He then just laid back and let the crane do the work. By the time he neared the doors of the shop he was nearly recovered. He made sure that the truck steered in correctly. Once the truck was in the shop the others remotely closed the door. After the door was closed it didn't take long for the heaters in the shop to warm everything up. They rushed out after they felt like it was safe to check on Mason. He was just exiting the truck as they reached him.

Lea almost knocked him down slamming into him with a hug.

He squeezed her back real tight and said, "I love you too, sis."

Ernest put his hand on his shoulder and said, "You alright, son?"

"Yes, sir, I'm good, nothing a warm cup of coffee won't fix. Hey, let's not stand around here doing nothing, we've got a world to save. Let's get this thing unloaded and check it out."

Once they unloaded the Volan and got it next to a shop heater it thawed right up.

Reggie checked it out and said, "Yep, everything is fine. I didn't expect it to be damaged. I mean it goes through the Exterius of the sun."

"Good point," Ernest replied.

So, they got to work gathering everything they thought they might need from the Volan. Once they were done, they headed back to the lab.

As they walked back the four of them began to talk.

Ernest started with a thought. "I have a theory on time traveling with this new technology added to my machine."

"Okay, Ernest let's hear it."

"Well, Reggie, you have traveled through wormholes. So, follow me here. When you go through a wormhole, you may travel millions of miles in seconds. Right?"

"Yes."

"When you do this there is no effect on you. You pass through and come out the other side just the same as you went in. Now Volans use speed to travel through the wormholes. The time machine combined with the Volan, could possibly travel within the wormhole. So, you could theoretically travel into a wormhole and instead of passing through it, you could stay there."

"Okay, but why would you want to stay there?"

"My theory is if you don't change going through, then you won't change staying in it. So, if you left this second in our timeline here. Then stayed 100 years in a wormhole. You could return a second later here and not have aged. You'd only be one second older."

"Gramps, that sounds a little crazy to me."

"Well son, we are talking about time travel and wormholes. Plus, you're talking to your great grandfather from Venus and a man that had twins with his wife from the sun."

"That is a fair point."

"Ernest, I'm not sure. I mean in theory it works, but it would have to be tested."

"Uncle, I mean Grandpa Ernie, is this just a thought in passing or is this a thought in planning? Where are you headed with this?"

"I'm glad you asked. So, I think I can travel back in time, grab Martha right before she passes. I could go into a wormhole dimension with her, and she wouldn't age. So, we could spend a lifetime together. As long as I don't introduce her to this timeline, there would be no effect here. Now, I could potentially bring her to our current time and there shouldn't be an issue, other than she would begin to age again. I could pull Adeline out of some point in time, and she could spend more time with her mother. Then return her a second later and she'd still be the same age."

"Gramps, you're making my head hurt."

"It is a lot to take in, but I do think it would work."

"Ernest, it sounds plausible. I think it could work, but again I'm not sure. I think we need to get the situation at hand fixed first though."

"Absolutely. I totally agree."

Mason asked, "So what's the plan there? We just go back in time and convince you to not make the time machine in the first place?"

"No, I think I need to do this on my own."

"Grandpa Ernie, you've done things by yourself for so long. You don't have to do this alone."

"I'm sorry, I meant the time traveling. I unquestionably need all of your help with preparing everything."

Reggie interjected, "So, if you fix everything and return to this time, none of us will remember anything that happened today. Well, nobody but you."

"I thought about that, and I have gained too much today to lose it. I now have two grandchildren that know who I really am. Also,

I have gained a true friend, that though I cost him everything, he showed compassion and didn't hold it against me."

"How do you propose we remember if we don't go with you?"

"Well, we can recalibrate the butterfly net so that it keeps everything the same in the lab. As long as you all stay in the lab until I return, then you should all remember today."

"Okay, that may work."

Mason stepped in, "That still doesn't tell me how we're going to fix all of this."

"Yes, to answer that. I will go back just before the first time that I time traveled. I will recalibrate the butterfly net at that point in time so that it will "autocorrect" everything. Though, I will allow it to generate the lightning storms so that Reggie still comes to earth to help Lea. That way the sequence of events stays the same. "

"I'm going to need ibuprofen before this is over."

As they continued to walk Lea asked about Ernest and Martha. "Did Grandma Martha know that you were from Venus?"

"Of course, we kept no secrets."

"Would you mind telling me how you two met?"

"I'd love to tell you. I remember it like it was yesterday, although it was 1924. Fortius and I had not long arrived on one of our trips. We were walking around Galveston, taking in the sights, and we decided to make our way to the beach to just sit and relax. I always enjoyed the ocean breeze. As we sat there gazing over the ocean, I saw something out of the corner of my eye. There she was, her strawberry brown hair glistening in the sun. Her blue eyes were as blue and bright as the blue stars of Orion. Her smile and laugh were captivating. She walked along the beach wearing a blue dress with yellow and white flowers, eating an ice cream cone, talking with one of her friends. In all my years I had not seen anything as beautiful as she. I was mesmerized by her, just lost in her beauty. Then Fortius bumped me and said, 'Don't just stare at her like a weirdo, go talk to her." So, I did. She was 21, and we instantly fell in love. We married a year and a half later. Fortius was my best man at the wedding. In 1928 we had our beautiful little girl, Adeline Grace. Martha was a wonderful wife and mother. The rest as they say is history."

"You really loved her, didn't you?"

"I still do."

Soon they arrived in the lab.

"Okay, everyone, let's get to work. Lea and Reggie, can you check my calculations on the butterfly net and see where I miscalculated? Mason, if you would help me with the time machine and getting everything hooked up correctly."

They all went feverishly to work at their assignments. Reggie and Lea typing on the keyboards sounded like a stampede of horses as they were trying to rapidly come up with a solution.

Ernest and Mason were using power tools to speed the process. *Zimp, zimp, whirl, whirl, bratatat,* the tools went.

Ernest was instructing Mason on what to do. "Okay son, take that blue part off there and put the orange one in its place. Okay unplug that and plug it here. Take that and pass it to me."

Mason stopped and asked, "Can I name this thing? I'm tired of calling it the time machine. I think it needs a name because it's no longer just a time machine. It's a ship. One that we are hoping will help us get out of the situation we are in."

"Okay son, what do you want to call it?"

"Exodus!"

"I think that is a fitting name, Exodus it is."

"WE FOUND IT!" yelled Lea. "It's a logic error. That's why it was so hard to find. It was right here in the source code. You simply assigned a value to the wrong variable. All I have to do is this and BAM, it's done. It'll work now. The butterfly net is now programmed and ready to go."

"That's my girl," said Ernest.

A larger-than-life smile came across her face as she beamed with the accomplishment of making her grandfather proud. They put the finishing touches on Exodus. Then it was time to go.

Mason commented, "Gramps, I still don't know why you want to go alone."

"Well, son, I just feel like this mess up, I need to fix. I know that you all could help, but sometimes you have to clean up your own mess."

"I guess I get that."

"I'll be back shortly."

"Funny."

"Okay, here we go. Fire up the butterfly net."

With that loaded up into Exodus. Lights started flashing around the machine just like before. The wind began to swirl as it sounded like the machine was picking up steam. Then FLASH, he was gone. The room settled back down, and it became eerily quiet.

Mason said, "I should have gone with him. This is creepy, and I can't even leave to get a cup of coffee."

Lea responded, "He'll be back soon. Don't worry, it'll all be fine."

"I know it'll be fine. I just don't like not being able to leave this room."

Soon the wind began to stir again, and lights began to flash. They saw Exodus appear. Then suddenly it disappeared once again.

"WHAT JUST HAPPENED?" Shouted Mason.

"I don't know, everything was hooked up right. I mean, we even reran the numbers before he left." Reggie replied.

"Then the wind began to stir again and the lights flashing. Slowly they could see Exodus appearing. Finally, it was back. The door opened and out stepped Ernest.

"I told you I would be right back."

"Gramps, you scared the daylights out of me, we didn't know what happened. It's like the machine tried to come back. Then it disappeared again. Then it was back again."

"Really? I'll have to look into that."

About that time Reggie's phone rang.

"Hey, my love, I wanted to check on you. Are you coming back home tonight, or will you be working all night? I'm just curious," Arliaya said.

"I'm coming home right now baby; I'll be there in a few minutes. It's so good to hear your voice. Are the boys in the bed? Never mind it's late of course they are. I'm leaving now."

He then turned to the others, "Y'all got this from here, right? I gotta go see my family."

Ernest replied, "Yes, by all means, go."

Lea chimed in, "Well, I guess that means everything is back to normal."

"I guess so," said Mason.

Ernest replied, "Well, maybe not exactly normal."

Lea looked at him, "What do you mean 'not exactly normal?' What is different?"

"I've kept too many secrets for too long. I will not keep secrets any longer. You know how the machine started appearing and then disappeared?"

"Yes."

"I did that. I did want to clean up my own mess, but I did have an ulterior motive. I knew that if I could come back into this time just enough that I could see you, then everything would be back the way it was supposed to be. That was priority number one. Once I had accomplished that, then I could test my wormhole time travel theory without affecting all of you. That's another reason I needed you all to stay. Because if I was wrong, I didn't want to harm anyone if it went wrong."

"Well, did it work? I mean I know you made it back, but otherwise? Did time work like you thought?"

"I'm going to say yes. I have actually been gone for years. Traveling in wormhole dimensions."

They both responded stunned, "WHAT?"

"Yes, plus I had company," he said as he turned towards Exodus with his hand lifted in presentation. "I'd like you two to meet your great grandmother, Martha."

Part 3
Life in the Wormhole

Life in the Wormhole Chapter 1

As the storm was raging, Martha was trying desperately to get out of the school building where she taught and back home to her family. She had gone up to the school to finish some last-minute things. She wasn't expecting the storm to get as bad as it was. The storm began to rage, and buildings were being demolished at this point. She got to the door to push it open, but the wind pushed too hard against her. The building she was in began to rock and reel. Things were looking more and more grim. She knew that this was most likely the end. Suddenly, lights began to flash in the center of the room and the wind began to stir within the building. She thought to herself this is "surely the end." About that time the Exodus appeared. She was almost more frightened by this than the storm outside. The door opened and a familiar face emerged.

"Ernie, is that you?"

"Yes, my dear, there is no time to waste, nor explain. Please, come with me now!"

With that she leapt towards him, he put his arm around her to move her quickly into the Exodus. When he got her safely inside, he hurriedly closed the door and started pushing buttons.

"Ernie, what is this contraption? Where is Adeline? Why does your hair have gray in it?

"I'll explain everything, my love. Just give me a few moments."

Soon they were off. They started to appear at Zindwhich for a brief moment.

"Who are those people?"

"Well, two of them are our great grandchildren. One is a colleague."

"Ernie, if this is another one of your pranks, I am not in the mood for it right now."

In a flash they were gone again.

"This is not a prank." He grabbed her hand and looked her straight in the eyes with tears beginning to run down his face. "I assure you; this is not a prank."

She ran her hand into his grayish silver hair and pulled his head to her shoulder. He began to weep bitterly as he pulled her into him and held her tightly.

"I've missed you so very much."

She held him for a moment. He then turned to the controls.

"There will be time later to catch up, all the time in the world."

With that he set their destination to a wormhole.

"Okay, my love. Now, I can explain."

"I died in the hurricane, you built a time machine to come back and save me?"

He tilted his head slightly. "You were always so smart."

"Sweetheart, how long have I been gone?"

Tears began to run down his face as he replied, "62 years."

"Oh, my poor Ernie. My poor, poor Ernie. Come here let me hold you."

They embraced and held onto each other as they wept. It seemed like an eternity.

Martha stepped back, "So seeing as we have great grandchildren, that I will have to meet. That tells me that Adeline made it through the storm fine.

"Yes, yes. She turned out to be a wonderful young woman. She met a nice young man towards the end of 1962. They married in the beginning of 1964. They had a beautiful daughter, her name is Martha, in 1965. Making her your age now."

"Oh dear, I missed so much. My age now? So, it's 2023? Oh, my lands. Tell me about her and our great grandchildren."

"Well, unfortunately I didn't get to play a huge part in their lives. I faked my death in 1973 when Martha was just 8 years old."

"So, you've been alone for nearly 50 years? My poor darling. You never told Adeline that you were from Venus, did you?"

"No, I just couldn't find a way or a time. Speaking of time. We are about to try a theory out. You know how I explained how Fortius, and I traveled through wormholes to make it to earth?"

"Yes."

"Well, I plan on putting the Exodus, that's what our great grandson named it."

"Oh, sounds like he reads his Bible, that's good."

"Yes, indeed he does. So, we're going to put the Exodus into a wormhole. I believe that neither of us will age there. We can travel the Galaxy and find new worlds and maybe even civilizations. We can make up for lost time."

She gently grabbed his arm and hugged it. "We were about to retire and travel the world. How much better to travel the worlds. Our great adventure."

"Yes, yes indeed." Ernest laid his head on the top of Martha's head as she stood holding his arm and he, her hand.

As they talked about everything from the Berlin wall coming down, the JFK assassination, the Civil rights movement, computer technology, landing on the moon, (which they shared a laugh over), cellphones, Wi-Fi, they tried to cover 62 years of information in one sitting.

He began to show her how to operate the Exodus and explain the extra gadgets. He had designed a teleportation belt that was linked to the Exodus. This was so if they were to get in danger while not close to the Exodus, they could by the push of a button be teleported into the Exodus. He had made jet packs to make traveling a planet easier. His design used a new hydrogen peroxide technology with air flow to propel through the air. He had made neck gear that by the push of a button would put an airtight shield over their faces. It had an oxygen converter that would read the atmosphere and produce oxygen from the outside air. As he was winding down explaining all the gadgets, Martha stepped in.

"You have thought of everything haven't you?"

"Probably not everything, but I've had many years to invent and prepare. So, I tried to cross every t and dot every I. Oh, there's one more thing. This bracelet is connected to the Exodus. It works on the same principle as the time machine. As long as we are in the time machine we don't age as we travel. This bracelet will work the same way and stop our aging as long as we are wearing them."

"So, if we take them off do we accumulate the years of aging at that point or do we just begin to age normally?"

"We would begin to age normally at that point."

"Good to know. So, how long are we traveling for?"

"I'm not sure. I thought we'd just travel until we decided to go home."

"Yes, I will eventually want to go home. I want to meet all of our grandchildren."

"Well, I have the Exodus programmed so all we have to do is push this blue button and it will take us right back to where you saw our grandchildren earlier. The exact second. So, we could be gone countless years and still not lose any time with them."

"Wonderful. So, where to first?"

They pulled up a radar that would detect planets and found the nearest one.

"That looks like a good one, Ernie, what do you think?"

"My love, as long as I'm with you, I'll go anywhere."

With a smile she responded, "Then let's go there."

As they cleared the clouds, they could see dense, lush forest everywhere.

There were beautiful mountains covered in trees. They landed and adorned their gear and exited the Exodus. As they did, Ernest clicked a button that made it invisible.

"See, like I said, you thought of everything."

Rainbows were scattered sporadically throughout the area as the magnificent waterfalls created them against the planet's sun. They fired up the jet packs to get a bird's eye view. It took a little time of clumsily bumping into things trying to get off the ground. Soon enough, though, they were off, flying high above the astonishing landscape. They heard something in the distance that seemed to be pushing its way through the landscape. *Crack, snap, pop,* went the trees, then *crash* a tree hit the ground. What emerged had them both astonished.

"Is that a dinosaur?" Exclaimed Martha.

"It appears to be. Though, I'm not sure what kind."

It resembled a tyrannosaurus rex. It

stood nearly 20 feet tall on its hind two feet, but its arms were longer. Long enough that once it cleared the tree line it got down on all fours. It was blue from the top of its head down its massive back to the tip of its tail. The rest of its body was a brownish color.

"What a magnificent sight," said Martha.

"Yes, indeed. We've apparently stumbled upon a prehistoric planet.

"Look over there."

There was another dinosaur that resembled an Ankylosaurus. Its back was blood red; it had a thin yellow line that ran around its body beneath the red and turned green from that point down. There were flying animals that looked more like giant red falcons than pterodactyls. There was a smaller animal that could walk around on its hind legs but would roll up into a ball to cover more ground or as a self-defense mechanism as its outer shell seemed to be hard as a rock.

They found large edible fruits and vegetables. A pear-shaped fruit that was red and white. A gourd shaped vegetable that was orange and yellow. Basketball sized purple fruit with little red spots. Each had its own delicious flavors.

Due to them being a scientist and a teacher, this planet was of great interest to them. They explored the planet, seeing many beautiful animals and sights. They kept journals, logging everything they saw. They made their lodging in a cave while they were there. This protected them and the Exodus from the large carnivorous animals. They spent only a couple months gathering information and observing the wildlife and habitat. It was a livable place, but it could be very dangerous with all the dinosaurs. They were very careful in this prehistoric planet that they called

"Elsewhere," but decided after their short time that it was time to move onto the next place.

So, they loaded up in the Exodus and off they were again. The next planet they arrived at was a Utopia, which is what they came to call it. This planet, much to their surprise, was uninhabited. It had beautiful beaches, mountains, trees, and wildlife. Though the wildlife here was more like that of earth. After much study of the planet, they decided this would be their home planet in the wormhole dimension. They built a simple cottage while they were there overlooking the ocean. When the wind blew in it reminded them of Galveston. They spent years here exploring the planet and enjoying being with each other. After some time, they decided it was time to explore a different planet. Though they hoped to find a civilization soon.

Unbeknownst to them they would find a large civilization very soon.

Life in the Wormhole Chapter 2

When they landed safely on the next planet, they were not prepared for what they would find. Everything on the planet was green and beautiful. Everything was also very, very large. They thought maybe this was another dinosaur planet. As they were exploring on the ground, they suddenly heard a deep roar of sorts. It did not sound like a ferocious roar. No, it was more of a broad lazy roar. They would soon find out that it was not a roar at all.

"What was that?" Asked Martha.

"I have no idea, but I think we're about to find out." Replied Ernest.

They could hear something that was definitely large approaching their location. Its footsteps seemed to shake the ground as it got closer. Soon, to their astonishment, what they could only describe as a giant stepped out into the clearing with them. He stood nearly 12 feet in height; his burly stature was draped in what seemed to be a furry animal skin type clothing. His large black hair and beard almost consumed his face.

They were so frightened they nearly pushed the buttons on their belts to return to the Exodus. Then he knelt on one knee and began to speak, freezing them to their spots.

"Now, aren't you a darlin' lookin' pair," he said with a strong accent.

"And where are you from, and how did you get here?

"Umm," said Ernest hesitantly. "We are travelers from another planet. We just arrived. We mean no harm."

"Ya ain't hurtin' nothing my friend. We don't mind da company. My name is Gorm."

"My name is Ernest, and this is my wife, Martha."

"Well, I'm pleased ta make your acquaintance Ernest and Martha. Ya should go wit me. I'm sure dat everyone would love to make your acquaintance."

"Well, I mean, if you insist." Ernest replied sheepishly.

"Ya ain't got nothing to fear. We be a peaceful people. We call ourselves the Velikan."

Martha whispered to Ernest, "He does seem polite, and we can always hit the buttons to transport back to Exodus."

"He does. His size is what frightens me."

"Let's go with him. You never know until you try."

With that they followed the giant through the woods. Although his one step was many for them. They were struggling to keep up and talk at the same time. Finally, he realized what was happening.

"Where are my manners? I didn't tink about how hard it might be on ya to keep up with me. Ya is welcome to ride on my shoulders. If you'd like."

They didn't really want to ride on his shoulders but felt like it'd be rude to refuse him. Out of trying to remain polite, they agreed. It did, admittedly, make their trip much easier. Gorm was quite the talker. He continued to talk all the way to the village, allowing them to take in their surroundings without having to give much input.

"Now, where is it ya say dat you're from?"

"We came here from earth, a planet in another galaxy."

"Hmm, sounds a bit interesting. How's far way dat be?"

"A very long way. You don't seem to be surprised by us being here. Do you have many visitors from other planets?"

"No sir, as far as I know ya be the first. De ting is do, I know dat de Creator is great. I just never tought He'd stop wit just us."

Martha replied, "That is a very good observation, Gorm. Not many people think that way."

"Dank you ma'am. I always try to remember how big and great my Creator is. Ah, here we are. Dis be our village."

As they entered the village, they could see giant sized houses everywhere. All wooden outsides with rooftops of grass or lapped wood. Every one of the dwellings that they could see had a chimney of stone peering over the top. As Gorm entered the village, everyone began to gather to meet his new friends.

"Everyone, dis is Ernest and Martha. They be from a place called earth. It's somewhere way away from here."

The giants began to gather around, greeting them with smiles.

Gorm stepped in front of the two and told the others, "Don't be crowding dem now. Dey be our guests, and we need to treat dem dat way." He began to introduce different people to them. "Dis is Jud and Aoife his wife. Dis is Cadal and Oisín, cousins dey be to each other. Eoin and, dat's enough. Ya can meet dem all later."

Gorm motioned for his wife, "Dis is my lovely wife, Edda. We'd be pleased to have ya stay wit us."

Edda reiterated Gorms invitation, "Yes we would love to have de two of ya stay. Dats if ya don't mind a little one."

With that their son little Gorm peered around his mother's leg shyly at them.

"Oh, aren't you just the most adorable little guy. Come here sweetheart, there's no need to fear us." Martha assured him.

With a little encouragement from his mother, he went to Martha and sat down in front of her. Martha began to play with him and talk to him. Soon they made their way to Gorm's home. They spent the night talking and learning about each other. Ernest and Gorm broke off in one conversation and the ladies did the same. Ernest and Gorm talked about how they used coal and steam power to run most of the mechanical type things on their planet. Ernest began to explain electricity to Gorm and told him he was sure that they could find a way for them to have it. While Martha and Edda were bonding over children and life in general. Soon it had crept into the morning hours. Edda prepared a place for Ernest and Martha to sleep. Then, they all bedded down for the remainder of the night.

Martha rolled over and looked at Ernest with a smile, "Ernie, I think we need to stay here awhile. I could form a school here and teach the children and even the parents if they'd like. I just feel like they need us."

"I'm glad to hear you say that. I was going to suggest the same thing. I think we can help them. I'd like to help them set up a power grid."

"It's settled then, we're staying in 'Gigantia'. I love you."

"So that's the name huh? I love you too. Goodnight. my love."

The next morning, they shared their decision with Gorm and his family who were delighted to hear this. They wasted no time in helping them build a home of their own. Gorm had suggested building it to fit their size, but Martha and Ernest insisted that it be big enough that they could have company over. They did, however, build them some furniture that was more their size. Their table sat on a larger table so that they could have visitors. They also built a school so Martha could teach. She had a platform that would elevate her to more of an eye level with her students.

Ernest began teaching about electricity to anyone that wanted to learn. He decided to use a steam turbine generator method to produce the power that they needed. Seeing as they already had an understanding of how steam worked, this would simplify the process. They made many friends with Velikan people. They truly were a kind, peaceful race. Little Gorm, who Martha called Little Gormy, took a real liking to Martha. So much so that he called her mum. His mother did not mind at all for she loved Martha as well. They became like sisters while Ernest and Gorm became like brothers.

It took nearly 30 years to build the electrical system and get it up and going completely. They did get it going, though.

And they did not stop there. Ernest helped design a flying ship capable of carrying many of the Velikan. It was a sight to behold. It was wrapped in a thick metal outer shell. It had an observation deck that went around the entire top of it. There was plenty of room below with lots of food storage and cabins to sleep in. Once complete, Martha named it the Ark. He also designed it so it could travel at great speeds. Although they had spent many years here it did not feel like it to them. They were so involved with everything and truly loved the Velikan people so much. They discovered areas that emitted natural gas during exploration, and so they utilized this for their civilization as well.

After many years Ernest and Martha decided that it was time to move on. On hearing the news Gorm and all the Velikan people prepared a great farewell celebration. Many laughs and many tears were shed as they reminisced through the night. The next day they arose and said their goodbyes.

Little Gormy lifted Martha up to him, she wrapped her arms as far as they would go around his massive neck.

"I'm going to miss you, my little Gormy."

Little Gormy, with tears streaming down his face said, "I'm goin to miss you to, Mum."

"Hey, we'll come back to visit. This isn't goodbye, just see you later."

"Yes ma'am."

They loaded up in the Exodus and prepared to leave. They were about ready to go home but thought they'd make one more quick stop. This stop though would not be anything like the others. This one was going to place them in grave danger.

Life in the Wormhole Chapter 3

It was not long after they left the Velikan people that they spotted a little planet that they thought they'd just make a quick stop in to see. They really did not want to stay long because they really wanted to get back to their family on earth. As they entered the atmosphere, they could tell there was something different about this planet. It was a very dark and dismal looking place. The ground looked cracked and dry. There were what looked like large fire pits everywhere. They could barely see some type of roadway as they neared the ground. They looked up towards the sky, and it was a dark red color. There were structures in the distance, but they could not make them out. As they landed and exited the Exodus, they felt an eerie feeling come over them.

As they began to walk, they could see a little village up ahead. They could see what looked like fire lanterns of some type in the windows of the cottages that looked more like mud huts. However, it did not look like anyone was actually in the village. Upon getting closer they could see shadows moving in the cottages. They approached one of the homes and knocked cautiously, with their hands on the transportation buttons. A long *squeak* sound, from the hinges was heard, as the occupant cracked the door slightly.

"What do you want?" A shaken voice came from the other side of the door.

Martha stated, "We mean you no harm."

"We've heard that before," said the voice behind the door.

"Truly, we don't."

The door began to open a little more. Then a figure appeared. It stood like a human, but it was pink all over. Its face had similarities to that of a human, but it had a larger nose and longer ears. It almost resembled a mole rat. It stood there with tattered clothing as it timidly looked down.

Martha said, "You can look at us. We won't hurt you."

It began to lift its face slightly to look at them.

"My name is Martha and what is your name?"

"Tim," he replied.

"Well, Tim, it's nice to meet you," she said as she extended her hand.

Tim slowly lifted his hand up towards hers. She gently took his hand, gave him a light handshake, and released his hand.

"Why are you so frightened?"

"Jardich, he is the tyrant that has enslaved our people. He crashes landed here from another planet. We did not have the materials he needed to repair his ship, so he decided to take advantage of us and appoint himself ruler over us. We are burrowers and live primarily underground. He built the fire pits you see to pump heat into the ground so that we could not escape him. He has this large scepter that has a blue glow on top that he will blast us with if we do not obey him. There were six men that arrived with him. They all are arrayed in black metal type armor, that seems to be impenetrable. They rule with iron fists, and they see all. I am personally surprised that they did not see you arrive."

An interruption came from behind Martha and Ernest.

"Oh, but we did," said one of the ironclad soldiers.

Tim slammed his door closed in terror leaving Martha and Ernest at the mercy of the soldiers.

"We saw you arrive and Jardich wants you to come with us."

Ernest stepping in front of Martha replies, "And what if we refuse?"

The soldier struck Ernest in the head with the club that he carried, immediately knocking him unconscious. The other soldier grabbed Martha by the arm, pulling her away from Ernest. She was now afraid to push the button on her belt that would return her to the Exodus because it would leave Ernest defenseless and alone. She screamed for help.

The soldier that had her arm turned her towards him and said, "Don't waste your breath. These cowards will not help you. You belong to us now."

With this, they transported the two of them to Jardich. Martha saw as they drew near a dark looking stone castle. It had huge wooden doors on the front with large black hinges and bars. As they entered the castle, they closed the doors behind them. It didn't take long for them to enter the presence of Jardich himself. He had a stature of 6' 5", was broad across the chest, and was wearing the black armor just like the other soldiers. He sat upon a stone throne with his scepter and a kingly type of cape was about his shoulders. Just then Ernest was coming back to.

Jardich lent forward and said, "That is no way to treat our guests. I apologize for my soldiers' zeal. They do as I say without question. Sometimes they can be a little rough. My name is Jardich, I am the ruler of this world. I would like to welcome you."

Martha responded, "If we are guests, then let us go. We want to leave this place."

"Now, I can't do that. You just got here!" He stood as he spoke, and his voice got sterner and fiercer, "I need to know how you got here because I need to get off of this useless piece of dirt. So, tell me, how did you come to our planet?"

Ernest nodded at Martha to push their buttons. They did, but nothing happened. Ernest realized quickly that whatever was powering Jardich's scepter was interfering with the signal somehow. He knew the only way for them to work was to get away from the scepter.

Ernest, trying to think quickly, said, "We were dropped off. Our ride will be back shortly. We must meet at the rendezvous point, but if they see anyone else there, they will not land."

"Oh, I see. You think me a fool! You come to my planet, where I am king, and try to lie to me? I'll tell you what. As a merciful king, I am going to make you a deal. I will keep the woman, and you bring me the ship. If you do not? Well, I'll simply have to vaporize her by turning my scepter to full power."

"NO!" Do not harm her! Let her go."

"Bring me the ship, and you can have her. Or don't, and I'll kill her."

Ernest stood straight; his demeanor changed. He stepped forward and said from the depths of his soul, "Never push a peaceful man to the point of violence. Do not harm my wife. You will not like what happens to you if you do."

"Little man, you are in no position to issue threats. Bring me the ship, and you're free to go. Now leave."

Ernest turned to Martha and said, "I'll be back, my love."

Then he left in haste. Once he was clear of the scepter, he quickly transported himself to the Exodus.

Martha addressed Jardich, "You call yourself a leader and these people cowards, but you hide behind stone walls with soldiers and weapons and threaten innocent people."

"I don't need your lectures."

"I just want you to know that you have made a grave mistake."

"I'll take my chances," he said with a chuckle, his callused heart and mind unphased.

As they waited for Ernest to return, two soldiers were standing on the inside of the castle near the large wooden doors. Suddenly, there was a loud **BOOM** against the doors that shook dust from all around the door

Jardich leaped to his feet, "What was that?"

Martha commented, "That is the sound of a peaceful man."

Again, there a **BOOOOM!** This one was louder, so loud that it began to crack the stones a little. Then with one more explosion of sound, the doors flew, hinges and all, all the way across to the middle of the room. In stepped Little Gormy and right behind him was Big Gorm, Jud, Cadal, Oisín, Eoin and Ernest. The two soldiers fainted at the size and number of the giants that stepped into the room. Jud scooped them up and tossed them into a bag that he hung over his shoulder. Little Gormy let out an enormous shout "MUM!"

Martha shouted back, "Over here!"

Jardich just looked at her with fear in his eyes. Little Gormy burst into the room, causing a slight tremor with every step, and seeing Jardich beside Martha ran straight for him like an angry bull. Jardich pointed his scepter at Little Gormy, but he just grabbed it in the palm of his left hand and crushed it to pieces. With his right hand, he grabbed Jardich, lifting him high off his feet and slammed him into the stone wall, cracking the wall and his armor simultaneously.

He got right up to his face and growled, "If you've hurt me mum, I'll crush you with me bare hands."

Then Little Gormy heard Martha's voice, "I'm okay, Gormy, you can put him down."

Gormy dropped him and carefully embraced Martha. The other four soldiers were still standing there frozen in fear by the presence of the Velikan.

Jud turned his bag upside down dumping the other two soldiers out like they were yesterday's trash. The rest of the Velikan put them all in a corner together.

Ernest stepped forward and addressed them, "You enslaved this planet, tormented it's people, and then you threatened my wife. You deserve to die. My wife has taught me many years to be merciful like Jesus. I've tried to follow the example set before me. But I don't always succeed. With that he pulled a sleek silver pistol, pointed at them all and pulled the trigger. *Zzzzzaaaappp,* it went then they were all gone.

Martha laid her hand on Ernest's arm, "Did you vaporize them?"

"I wanted to, I wanted to drop them on the face of the sun, but I didn't do either. No, I transported them elsewhere."

"Do you mean Elsewhere? As in the planet?"

"Yes, they should be having a prehistoric experience right about now."

Big Gorm chimed in, "Good one der me friend. Wit any luck one of dem lizards der will eat dem."

"Gorm." Martha said, shaking her head at him.

"Just saying if it 'appens den de Creator probably duaght it was a good idea." He said with a loud chuckle.

They all shared a laugh over this. They then informed the people of the planet that they were liberated. The Velikan snuffed out all of the fire pits. Ernest offered to take them to Utopia, but they politely declined. They could now burrow into the ground again, so they were content with staying there.

After repairing the doors of the Exodus, they bid their farewells and returned with their friends to Gigantia for a day. They wanted to let all their loved ones there see that they were safe. The next morning, they arose early to leave.

Martha turned to Ernest and said, "Let's go home, my love. We can travel again some other time."

"Agreed," he responded.

With that they were off. They began to appear back at Zindwhich, the very second that Ernest had planned for. Ernest exited the Exodus and Martha could hear him conversing with Reggie, Lea, and Mason. After Reggie's exit Ernest gave a short explanation to Lea and Mason.

Then he said, "Yes, plus I had company," and turned towards Exodus with his hand lifted in presentation, "I'd like you two to meet you great grandmother, Martha."

www.ingramcontent.com/pod-product-compliance
Lightning Source LLC
Chambersburg PA
CBHW072010150726
47999CB00002B/590